"I have no intention of running away again, Giles."

His eyes softened. "I am glad of that. My brother is very appealing, but you need someone more mature, more considerate. It is to be hoped"—he hesitated— "I hope you'll meet such a man."

Damaris found that she was holding her breath. A change seemed to have come over Giles. He was regarding her almost yearningly. As if . . . but no, she must be wrong.

"I must take you back to the house, my dear," Giles said abruptly. "Come."

Giles lifted Damaris into the saddle and sprang up behind her, slipping an arm around her waist and urging his horse forward. He held her firmly. Her head was against his chest, and she could hear the steady beati̶n̶g̶ ̶o̶f̶ ̶h̶i̶s̶ ̶h̶e̶a̶r̶t̶ ̶b̶e̶n̶e̶a̶t̶h̶ ̶h̶e̶r̶ ̶e̶a̶r̶.

"Giles . . ."

"Yes?"

"I do hope w̶e̶ ̶s̶h̶a̶l̶l̶ ̶b̶e̶ ̶f̶r̶i̶e̶n̶d̶s̶ again."

His encircling arm grew tighter. Was it merely by accident that he leaned forward so that his chin brushed against her curls?

"So do I, my dear."

Dear Reader:

As the months go by, we continue to receive word from you that SECOND CHANCE AT LOVE romances are providing you with the kind of romantic entertainment you're looking for. In your letters you've voiced enthusiastic support for SECOND CHANCE AT LOVE, you've shared your thoughts on how personally meaningful the books are, and you've suggested ideas and changes for future books. Although we can't always reply to your letters as quickly as we'd like, please be assured that we appreciate your comments. Your thoughts are all-important to us!

We're glad many of you have come to associate SECOND CHANCE AT LOVE books with our butterfly trademark. We think the butterfly is a perfect symbol of the reaffirmation of life and thrilling new love that SECOND CHANCE AT LOVE heroines and heroes find together in each story. We hope you keep asking for the "butterfly books," and that, when you buy one—whether by a favorite author or a talented new writer—you're sure of a good read. You can trust all SECOND CHANCE AT LOVE books to live up to the high standards of romantic fiction you've come to expect.

So happy reading, and keep your letters coming!

With warm wishes,

Ellen Edwards

Ellen Edwards
SECOND CHANCE AT LOVE
The Berkley/Jove Publishing Group
200 Madison Avenue
New York, NY 10016

Second Chance at Love®
REGENCY

THE DASHING GUARDIAN
LUCIA CURZON

**SECOND CHANCE AT LOVE
BOOK**

THE DASHING GUARDIAN

First edition published May 1983

First printing

"Second Chance at Love" and the butterfly emblem are trademarks belonging to Jove Publications, Inc.

Printed in the United States of America

Second Chance at Love books are published by
The Berkley/Jove Publishing Group
200 Madison Avenue, New York, NY 10016

Prologue

PING!

Awakened out of a deep sleep by a sound of unknown origin, Damaris Vardon sat up in bed, her eyes on the windows facing her. The draperies were drawn back in order to allow her a view of the night sky.

Ping!

"There," she whispered. "'Tis a pebble. I am sure it's a pebble, and if so . . ." Wasting no more time in fruitless speculation, she slipped from the bed and, dashing to the windows, stared down into the street. A full moon shone on the spear-tipped rails of the high iron fence encircling Lord Harwine's London town house and made the gold epaulets gleam on the broad shoulders of a gentleman standing below. His arm was raised, evidently

1

with the intention of launching another missile.

Damaris's heart, which had been in the region of her toes when she had retired, shot to its rightful position in her body.

"Robert," she whispered ecstatically. She leaned out of the window. "You're here," she called softly.

"Indeed I am!" He waved at her. "You've been a time coming to the window, but you do fill it beautifully, my dearest love."

"I was asleep."

"Hmmmm, a fine homecoming, I must say, with all the house shut up as tight as a drum and none to unlock the gates!"

Damaris leaned farther out of the window. "We were all primed to see you...since *early* morning," she stressed, "and your Mama gone sobbing to bed because she is sure something happened to you on the road, and neither your Papa nor Giles could persuade her differently."

"Giles," Robert echoed in tones of great dislike. "I presume my prig of a brother's used this occasion to discredit me the more?"

"Why are you so late?"

"Matters beyond my control. I—"

"That actress?" Damaris interrupted, swallowing a large lump in her throat.

"Damaris! I told you that was at an end," he replied indignantly. "I'd prove it to you, if you'd come down and let me in."

"Oh, Robbie," she cried, "is it still the same?"

"Is it the same with you?" he countered half-sternly. *"Forever!"*

"Oh, my own dearest darling, come and let me in."

Damaris drew back hastily. She felt almost faint with happiness. When she had gone to bed that evening, she had been almost positive that Robert, whom she had known for all but three of her eighteen years, had forgotten the words he had spoken to her on the occasion of his last leave, seven months ago. As she groped for the tinderbox, which was somewhere on the mantel, that glorious moment of mutual discovery came back to her.

She had been in the garden at Harwine's Keep, the family estate in Somerset, picking roses for Lady Harwine, who was feeling poorly. Robert had come striding along the path and had stopped and stared at her as if he had never seen her before.

"I vow, but you've become a beauty, my dear," he had said with amazement.

She had regarded him with equal astonishment. She had been used to his teasing since her parents' death, when she had come to live in the household of her guardian, Lord Harwine, Viscount Croy. Robert, his younger son, had been but five at the time of her arrival, and they had been raised as brother and sister. He and his sister Mary, aged six, had been her friends from the beginning; but as they grew older, Damaris had been Robert's shadow. With him she had gone hunting after rabbits, ridden pell-mell through the woods adjoining the estate, gone swimming in its lake, and taken part in his various pranks. Later, she had been privy to most of his confidences and knew about his passion for an actress at Drury Lane as well as for an opera dancer, the latter entanglement proving very costly to his family. Indeed, they had sighed with relief when he had joined the cavalry and gone off to Spain. Only his Mama, Damaris, and Mary had mourned his departure. In spite of his "wild oats," Damaris had long ceased to have sisterly feelings for him. Long before that moment in the garden, she had loved her old playmate deeply and hopelessly. And then he had come to stand next to her and said, "You've become very, very beautiful, little Damaris."

"Not beautiful," she had contradicted. "I've dark hair

and brown eyes and my skin, despite lemon washes—"

"Is golden and your hair blue-black and your eyes deep pools of darkness into which a man could fall and drown. I've been told there was a Vardon wed a Portuguese beauty who came to England in the train of Catherine of Braganza."

"Hundreds of years ago." She pouted.

"Not so. Not more than a hundred and fifty years—not that it matters when she lived. All that matters is that she's bequeathed to you a most exotic beauty. In fact, I think you are the loveliest creature I've ever seen."

The roses had fallen from her nerveless grasp and Robert had knelt to gather them. Smiling at her, he had said, "Behold, I am at your feet and like to remain there."

"You must not tease me so," she had chided half-tearfully.

"I am not teasing," Robert had protested huskily. "I wish only that I were not off to Spain tomorrow."

"But you'll return—you must," Damaris had whispered.

"Yes, I must," he had agreed, rising and putting his hands on her shoulders. "Damaris, do...do you care for me?"

"I love you. I've loved you all my life!"

"As a brother?"

"Never!"

"Oh, Lord," he had groaned. "I've been home near a month and until this moment...Oh, Lord, I do love you and...and to think I might have had these feelings for you for years and never known it."

"That's not possible," Damaris had said punctiliously. "There was Miss Malvina George at Drury Lane and Mademoiselle Yvonne and—"

He had slipped a hand over her mouth. Half-laughing, half-ruefully, he had exclaimed, "They were nothing. What I feel for you, my beautiful innocent, is quite, quite different. I shall come back to you!"

There had been only one more passionate encounter with him. That night he had slipped into her room and given her her first kiss, an experience that had filled her with an excitement she had never known before. She had clung to him, wanting him to kiss her again and again, but he had moved away, saying regretfully, "We must be careful, my love. You know I'm in my brother's black books, and with my father so ill, he's appointed himself surrogate head of the family."

"I hate Giles!" Damaris had said angrily. "'Tis a great shame that his fiancée was killed. If he were married, he'd be living away from us."

Robert had sighed. "We cannot change the past. I would give my eyeteeth not to have become involved with that wretched Yvonne. I cared nothing for her, and to think that she dared to . . ." He had frowned and sighed again. "But no matter, my angel. Even Giles will have forgotten the incident by the time I return, and then we shall see what we shall see. Meanwhile, let this be our secret."

"Oh, I shall," Damaris had promised ecstatically.

After Robert had gone and she had looked back on those brief moments, as she had over and over again in the seven months he had been away, Damaris could scarcely believe she had not dreamed them. One could not fall in love so quickly, she had assured herself. These feelings had been reinforced by the fact that he had written only twice, and though both letters had been full of protestations of his affection for her, they had also been spaced over half a year. Of course, he had been in the midst of the fighting and had been decorated for bravery as well as being promoted to first lieutenant. Still, she could not help but consider that he was in a country full of golden-skinned, dark-eyed beauties who, according to all reports, did not disdain to fraternize with British soldiers. Given Robert's susceptible nature and the distance that stretched between them and . . . But now he was back, and how ardently he had gazed at her. Yet, in no more than a fortnight he would be off to war again and so far away! Canada and America!

Damaris bit back a sob, and, finding the tinderbox, struck the flint and lighted the candle by her bed. Slipping into her pegnoir, she ran a brush through her tangled curls. Then, taking the candle, she tiptoed into the dark, silent hall. It was well past midnight, and everyone in the house was mercifully asleep; even Giles, who often had a line of light under his door long after his parents had retired. Damaris made a little face in the direction of his chamber.

All during the years she had spent in her guardian's house, Giles had been aloof. Indeed, as children, she, Robert, and Mary had called Giles and his older sister Deborah "the enemy," though the term applied mainly to him. A gulf of six and seven years lay between the two older children and Robert. Even at eleven, Giles had taken himself very seriously, not hesitating to reprimand his younger siblings when he felt they deserved it. He had not changed, but of course he was the heir. He was also getting old—nearly twenty-seven—and such a stick!

Damaris went down the stairs praying she would not step on the board that creaked. It lay in the middle of the sixth—or was it the seventh step from the top? If she had not been holding the candle, she would have slid down the banister—but, in the present circumstances, that would have been folly!

She reached the bottom of the two long flights with no mishap and had equal success in unbolting the door quietly. In a few moments, she had opened it, and, taking a key from the hall table, she ran down the flagstoned walk to the gates and handed it to Robert, who let himself in swiftly, closing and locking the gates behind him. Following Damaris into the house, he picked up the candle she had left on the table, and, placing his finger against his mouth, pointed to the stairs. Once they had reached the first floor, he seized her hand and pulled her into the library.

"Here," Damaris whispered. Taking the candle, she lit a pair of candelabra on the mantel, and immediately the room grew much lighter. "There," she whispered.

"Yes, there." Robert moved to her and enfolded her in his arms. "Oh, my Imp," he said, using the nickname he had given her years ago. "Oh, my own, I have missed you so dreadfully."

"And I have missed you, Robert...Robbie." She clung to him, as she had the night he had come to her room, and again he released himself gently from her embrace. "That's enough, my dearest."

"It's not...it's not," she whispered. Fearfully, she added, "You've changed. There's someone else, or perhaps it's still Malvina George."

"Malvina George," he echoed softly. "I'd forgotten the name. All these months I've thought only of you, dreamed only of you, my darling, and that's why I dare not go on kissing you, else I should not want to stop."

"I do not want you to stop, and if you loved me..."

"Ah, my sweetest, you are such an innocent. If I loved you less, I'd take you here. But as I am a man of honor, I cannot. As a man of honor, if I cannot have you as wife, I cannot have you at all."

Damaris barely heard what he was saying—or rather she had heard only the one word that had blotted out all the rest. "Wife," she repeated. "You...want to marry me?"

"With all my heart," he said fervently. He looked at her anxiously. "Yet this love of ours is something so new, perhaps you'll think it too soon for us to contemplate such a step."

"Too soon? No."

"Think on it, my darling, before you give me any answer. Sleep on it."

"I do not need to sleep on it," Damaris returned passionately. "You may believe my love for you has been a sudden thing, but it's not true. I've loved you for *such* a long time. Today, when you did not come, I thought...I feared..." She paused. "Why did you not come when you were expected?"

He laughed softly, fondly. "My dearest, I'm thinking we must exchange eyes."

"Exchange eyes?"

"Mine are green, but yours should be. You are still dwelling on Miss Malvina George, who has been gone from my memory ever since I replaced her with you."

Damaris caught his hand and pressed a kiss upon it. "I'm not jealous. I was worried about you. Mary's husband and most of the regiment arrived before noon."

"I did not come with them. I started earlier than they did, hoping to be here hours before. Unfortunately, my horse cast a shoe, and there was not a blacksmith within miles. So much for your actresses, Imp." He put an arm around her and drew her against him once more. "I've changed my mind, Damaris. I cannot wait longer for your answer. Will you marry me?"

"Oh, yes...oh, yes, yes, yes!"

"Oh, my love." He kissed her again. Almost shyly, he added, "Do you think it would be too much of a burden on you if we were to wed before I set sail for Canada?"

"A burden...no, no, no, I would wed you tonight, were it possible. Oh, Robert, I wish you did not need to go. I wish Giles were your younger brother and the one destined for the army."

Robert emitted a crack of laughter. "Lord, Lord, you'd not be wishing my precious brother upon us. We'd lose the war for certain!"

"Oh, you shouldn't say that," Damaris protested. "I do not think Giles is a coward."

"What?" Robert frowned. "Have you and the 'enemy'

turned allies then?"

"Never," Damaris protested passionately. "We never, never could be. He disapproves of me dreadfully. He's always reading me homilies on my behavior."

Robert laughed. "Have you been behaving badly in my absence, Imp?"

"I do not think so. I do not think it wrong to ride races with Mary through the Park. We did it at the Keep."

"Ah, but home is home and Hyde Park—" He broke off, startled, as the library door was suddenly thrust open by a tall man in a long brocade dressing gown.

"Oh!" Damaris cried. To her startled gaze it seemed as if the intruder had eyes of flame, but of course it was only the reflection of the candle he carried.

"Good evening, brother." Robert moved away from Damaris.

Giles bent a censorious eye upon him. "Might I ask what you are doing down here at this unseemly hour?"

"That is hardly what I should term a proper greeting after my seven months in Spain," Robert observed.

Damaris, who had been aware of a sinking feeling in the region of her chest, could only admire her lover's sangfroid. Looking from brother to brother, she was amazed, as always, by their close resemblance. Though Giles was definitely the taller of the pair, both had chestnut hair that curled around their broad foreheads. Both had green eyes, tip-tilted at the corners. Both had clefts in their square chins and each had a wide full-lipped mouth. But that was where the likeness stopped. The difference in their temperaments had marked their faces. Where Robert had a pleasant expression and was rarely without a smile, Giles presented the world with a stern, closed countenance. Of course, he had suffered an early grief when the beautiful, reckless Lady Laura Crowell, to whom he was to have been wed within the fortnight, had attempted a jump that everyone had pronounced far too high. Both she and her horse had fallen, the beast rolling on top of her and killing her instantly. Still, that had been four years earlier, and one could hardly wear the willow for so long. And it was certainly unfair to take one's grief out on everyone in the household! These thoughts had chased each other through her active mind so rapidly that Damaris was able to speak before Giles had an opportunity to give his brother the set-down for which he was so obviously primed. "Poor Robert was locked out, and I let him in."

"I see," Giles responded glacially. "And, having performed this act of mercy, it would seem to me 'twere better you retired to your chamber, Damaris."

"Yes, 'tis time and past," Robert agreed with a quelling glance at her. "We were but passing the time of day— or night, but it's best we meet tomorrow, my dear."

"Yes, I agree," Damaris said with feigned docility. She managed to keep the excitement from her tone. "We'll speak in the morning."

Taking her candle, Damaris added, "I'll bid you good night, Giles."

"Good *morning,* my dear," he remarked pointedly.

"Good morning, then," she murmured obediently and passed swiftly through the room.

Closing the door behind her, Damaris shook her head. Undoubtedly, Giles would give poor Robert a strong set-down, but Robert was used to that. It would be wonderful when she and Robert had their own household. That would not happen until he returned from the wars, but perhaps when Lord Harwine consented to their marriage, they could go away as Mary had with Sir Francis Gresham when they were wed. Then she and Robert would be together, and Giles could never interfere again!

Two days after Robert's arrival, he and Damaris stood side by side in front of the library desk. Behind it sat

Lord Harwine, clad in his dressing gown. In spite of the
fine weather, he was wrapped in shawls. A man of sixty,
he looked far older than his years. Since the onset of his
illness, he had lost a great deal of weight. His skin hung
loosely on his large frame, but in contrast was drawn
taut across his face, so that the ridges of his bones were
easily apparent. His eyes were darkly circled, and there
were deep lines of pain about his mouth. Though he sat
upright in his chair, he seemed to be holding himself
erect by sheer strength of will. Giles, standing beside
him, had an anxious look for his father. There was also
anger mirrored in his eyes which, Damaris thought resentfully, was directed at Robert.

Giles had always disliked his brother. For if Giles
were his father's favorite son, Robert was certainly his
mother's favorite. In the past two days, he had spent a
great deal of time closeted in the chamber she rarely left.
Lady Harwine's constitution, which was never strong,
had been ruined by the bearing of seven children in rapid
succession, as well as by the added agony of seeing three
of them perish almost as quickly. Her health had not
been improved by her worry over her husband.

Damaris stifled a sigh. She scarcely remembered her
own parents and had long been accustomed to look upon
her guardian and his wife as her real family. It was an
agony to see them both so ill. She wished that Lord
Harwine had consented to interview them in his bedchamber, but that was not his way. He conducted all
matters of importance in the library, and certainly this
was a matter of great importance—his consent to their
formal betrothal and speedy wedding. They would also
require his help to procure the special license they needed
to marry within the week. The week! It seemed incredible
that they would be wed so quickly and...Damaris paused
in her ruminations. Lord Harwine had cleared his throat.

Damaris fastened her gaze upon him. He looked very

grim, but that, of course, was because he was in such pain. Still, Damaris wished he bore a happier expression. Lady Harwine had been delighted at the thought of their nuptials and had readily given them her blessing.

"My, my, it seems only yesterday that you came here, Damaris, after your dear parents... and your Mama so beautiful... You have something of the look of her though she was fair. Your Papa was dark like you. Such a distinguished man. Such a tragedy that they were lost in that horrid storm off Brighton. But at least they died together. I could not imagine existence without dearest Athol."

"So you believe you wish to marry," Lord Harwine said, effectively scattering Damaris's second flock of thoughts.

"Yes, Papa," Robert acknowledged.

"And you'd have me believe this affection you share for each other is of long duration?"

"A year, Papa." A touch of tension had crept into Robert's tone.

"I see. A year during which you have spent most of your time in Spain."

"Yes, Papa, but—"

Lord Harwine held up an almost transparent hand. "And will soon be leaving for America?"

"Yes, Papa." Robert nodded. "In twelve days' time. That is why—"

Again Lord Harwine held up his hand. "I am aware of that." He shook his head. "And my answer to you is that I cannot permit it."

Robert stared at him incredulously. His face was flushed, his eyes brilliant with anger. "And why not?" he demanded hotly.

Damaris, too, shot an incredulous look at her guardian. She felt almost as if he had struck her. "Why not?" she echoed.

"For many reasons." Lord Harwine's sunken eyes settled on Robert's face. "You've been in love many times and have recovered from that—er—tender passion as quickly," he said sternly. "How can you be sure that you'll not—"

"But this is different, sir," Robert burst out. "This is not any paltry affair. I love Damaris and she loves me."

"It's true." Damaris felt tears start in her eyes. "I love him more than life!"

"Life." Lord Harwine snorted. "You know nothing about life."

"It's not true." She stamped her foot. "I—"

"Damaris," Giles interrupted coldly. "Do not treat my father to your histrionics. Surely you can see he is not well!"

Lord Harwine had a brief smile for him. "Do not worry, Giles. I am able to deal with them. I'm not yet on my deathbed."

"Nor will be for a long time, sir," Robert assured him.

"Be that as it may," Lord Harwine continued, "I cannot countenance this match. Damaris is just out of the schoolroom. She's seen nothing of the world."

"That does not matter," Damaris began, but paused as she received a quelling look from Giles.

"It *does* matter, my dear," Lord Harwine said firmly. "Moreover, I'll not have it said I brought up an heiress only to wed her to my son. It savors far too much of coercion."

"Does it not matter that we love each other?" Robert demanded.

"Yes, it does matter," Lord Harwine agreed. "And if, on your return to England, you are of the same mind, I'll not withhold my consent."

"But supposing I do not return?" Robert had an anguished look for Damaris.

"Oh, no!" she moaned.

"If you do not survive this war, you'd scarcely like to leave this child a widow," Lord Harwine said sternly.

"I *want* to be his widow!" Damaris cried hotly. And then, as the import of her words came home to her, she threw herself against Robert, clinging to him and sobbing desperately. "No, no, no . . . that's not what I meant."

Robert put a trembling arm about her. "We know what you meant, my darling." He faced his father. "Can you not see what this is doing to her—to both of us? I pray you, sir, let us marry and enjoy such happiness as might come to us before I must leave."

Lord Harwine shook his head. "No, my boy, I cannot for conscience sake consent to it. All that must wait until your return."

"But—" Robert began desperately.

"Robert," Giles said coldly, "you must consider this interview at an end."

Robert glared at him. "You chose to question my honor on the night I came home and accused me of impropriety, merely because Damaris let me in and lingered for a moment to welcome me. I see that you have poured your poison in our father's ear."

Lord Harwine looked at him in some surprise. "I knew nothing of any such incident. Giles had nothing to do with my decision," he added. "Your own past actions were what weighed with me, Robert."

"But they are past, sir."

"I'll need more proof than that," Lord Harwine told him crisply. "This war with the Americans, 'tis a sad mistake. I cannot believe it will last long. Indeed, I give it no more than six months." He turned to Damaris. "If you still wish to marry Robert when hostilities are at an end, I'll not stand in your way."

"I shall wish it," she cried. "I shall love him forever." Turning, she sped from the room.

"And 'tis the same with me." Robert strode after her,

joining her in the hall.

"Oh, R-Robbie," Damaris wailed, holding out her arms to him.

He embraced her tightly. "My love, my dear love," he whispered. "We'll not put a period to this, not yet."

"But he said—"

"Mama shall speak for us," he told her firmly. "He'll listen to her. I swear to you that before I sail for Canada, we will be wed."

The small clock on the mantel chimed one o'clock in the morning. Damaris cast a half-fearful, half-elated glance at the door. In other circumstances, her heart would have been heavy indeed, for it was Robert's last night at home and it might be years before they saw each other again. If only he had been able to convince his father that he had changed. But luck had not been with them. After that fateful interview in the library, Lord Harwine had taken a turn for the worse, which Giles blamed on them, chiding Damaris for her outbursts and Robert for pursuing his arguments when he knew that Lord Harwine never went back on his decisions. Lady Harwine, too, had been censorious. All in all, it had been an extremely trying period. His mother had been in tears and needed Robert to comfort her for hours on end. Lord Harwine was resting easier now and had been for the past two days. Yesterday Robert had approached Damaris. A thrill of excitement and anticipation went through her as she recalled his words.

"My darling, let me come to you tomorrow night. I love you so desperately. I cannot leave without being with you at least once before I die."

"Oh, I pray you'll not speak of dying," she had moaned.

"May I come to you?"

"Oh, yes, yes, of course, you must."

"My sweetest angel, I love you so much."

"And I you. I have been in agony," she had sobbed.

"Hush, my darling, we'll be together, but we must take care. I shall come to you after they're all asleep."

It was late. Damaris yawned and flushed. She was not sleepy. She could not be sleepy when Robert was coming to her. Yet she wished she had not drunk so much wine at dinner that night—Robert's farewell dinner. She choked back a sob and tensed when she heard a sound at her door.

Damaris hurried to open the door. Peering into the darkness, she did not see anyone. Where was Robert? She was about to close her door when it was taken from her grasp, and Robert hurried inside. He was wearing a dressing gown. At his throat, she glimpsed the frill of his nightshirt.

"My own love," he whispered, closing the door softly behind him.

"Oh, Robbie." She held out her arms.

He did not embrace her. Instead, he lifted her up and bore her back to the bed, where he put her down gently. A few seconds later, the mattress creaked under his weight as he stretched out beside her. "At last," he said in a low voice as he pulled her into his arms.

His chest was bare. Damaris was surprised and a little taken aback. "You're not—"

"Not what, my love?"

"Your s-shirt and r-robe . . ."

"Will soon be joined by your nightshift, love. Come, you must doff it."

"I . . . must . . ." She faltered.

"Yes." There was a touch of impatience in his tone. "There must be naught between us, my pretty innocent. Let me help you."

There was an upheaval in the bed as Robert eased Damaris's shift up toward her head. She did not know how he accomplished it so quickly, but all of a sudden she lay naked beside him. Even though it was dark in the room, she was hot with embarrassment.

She bit down a cry as she felt his hands on her breasts and then they moved over her belly to the softness at its base. She protested softly as his fingers suddenly invaded her most private parts. He was touching them, and she felt so very peculiar! She wanted to protest and move away but could not because he was Robert and she did not want to hurt his feelings. His mouth was on her mouth, but it was not a usual kind of a kiss at all. It was hard and hurtful. His tongue was in her mouth, and that was very strange. She was not sure she liked it, but before she could make up her mind, he was kissing her forehead, her cheeks, her throat and then he bit the soft flesh of her neck.

"Oh!" She could not restrain a moan.

"Did I hurt you, my love?" Robert murmured. "I did not mean to hurt you, only to taste your beautiful little body." His lips fastened on her nipples. Then he was biting them, and that hurt, too.

"Please!" Damaris whispered, pleadingly.

"Yes, yes, my love," His mouth was on hers again, and she was feeling odd because now the whole weight of his body was on top of her, pressing her down. She did not know whether she was excited or frightened or both. Robert was very excited. He was breathing hard and beginning to move back and forth while his hands kneaded her breasts. It was all so different than she had anticipated. She wished he would be gentler.

Then—of a sudden—she heard a sound and all the pressure ceased and Robert was away from her, rising from the floor where someone had thrust him. Raising her head, she blinked at a candle flame and saw Giles. He was wearing his long brocade dressing gown, the same one he had worn two weeks ago when he had come into the library. He set the candle on her night table and in a low, angry voice said, "Damn you to hell, get out of here!"

Robert was on his feet and coming at him, his fists clenched, only to halt as Giles added icily, "If you do not go peacefully, I'll awaken Father and tell him what you've done."

"Noooo!" Damaris moaned.

Robert did not answer. He flung himself at Giles, throwing him to the floor and leaping toward the fireplace where he seized a poker and rushed at the fallen Giles.

"No!" Damaris jumped out of bed. Covering Giles's body with her own, she cried, "No, you cannot, Robert. He's your brother!"

Swiftly, Giles rolled away from her and rose just as Robert, grabbing his robe, threw it about him and strode from the room. Giles followed. Crawling miserably back into bed, Damaris released a torrent of anguished tears.

The clock was striking. Damaris counted dully one, two, three, four, five. It was five o'clock in the morning on the day her fate would be decided. She did not doubt that Giles would tell Lord Harwine all that had happened. And Robert—what of him? "Oh, Lord." She buried her face in her pillow again. She was frightened, frustrated and confused. And then the door was being pushed open and her name whispered.

Damaris sat up in bed. "Robert?" she called softly.

He entered swiftly, clad in his scarlet uniform. Her heart turned over. "Robert," she sobbed. "You're leaving."

He nodded, turning a chastened face toward her. "I've come to say farewell, my own dear love." He knelt by the bed. "And to ask your forgiveness."

"My . . . forgiveness?" She faltered.

"Last night 'twas madness. I never should have tried to take advantage of your innocence."

"But I wanted it. I wanted you," she cried.

He stroked her hair back from her tearful face. "I wanted you too, but 'twas wrong of me. I did not stop to consider consequences. 'Twas only that I love you so much."

"And I love you—with all my being."

He looked down at her soberly. "If that is true, may I hope you'll wait for me?"

"Forever."

He laughed softly, but his voice cracked in the middle. "You'll not need to wait so long, my own. Your promise will keep me from all harm." Moving back, he pulled a seal ring from his finger. "Let this plight our troth."

"Oh, Robert," she protested, "that was the gift of your grandfather. 'Twas supposed to bring you luck in battle."

He laughed again. "Do you suppose I believe in such fancies? Your love is my luck." He slid the ring on her finger. "Lord, it would not fit two of your little fingers together."

"I shall wear it about my neck."

"'Tis not large enough for that," he teased.

"Silly, I'll hang it on a chain. There's one in my jewel box."

"An excellent solution." He pressed a kiss on her lips. "And now, farewell, my own."

She clutched him. "Oh, Robert, I cannot bear to have you go!"

"I must." He disengaged himself reluctantly from her hold. "Fare you well, Damaris." He hurried swiftly from the room.

Moments later, Damaris, kneeling at her window, saw him ride off. As she had hoped, he looked toward her windows and waved. She waved back and remained waving until all that remained to mark his passing was a cloud of dust upon the street. Her tears returned then, and, running back to her bed, she buried her head in the pillows. Yet there was another knock on her door. Tensing, she sat up.

"Yes?"

The door opened and Giles, dressed neatly in riding apparel, stood on the threshold. "I must speak to you," he said coldly.

Damaris glared at him. "Go away."

He shook his head. "No, I must speak."

"There's naught to say!"

"You saved my life last night, there's that to say. I thank you."

"He would not have—"

"On the contrary, I am sure he would have. His temper's always gotten the best of him. His passions, too, are strong, but he tells me he did not succeed in his intent. You had a narrow escape."

"I did not want to escape from him!" she flared. "Why did you come?"

"If I'd not come, you might have found yourself with child and none to father it," he told her harshly. "A child with a child—no good could come of that."

"I'm not a child. I am a woman grown, and I love him!" she cried furiously.

"You are even more of a child than I'd believed you to be. And today, my dear, you'll go to the country, where you'll stay until you've convinced me differently. I'll tell my father that you need a change of air. And I suggest that you do not run to him with any protests or trouble my mother with them, either."

"What will you tell them?" Damaris demanded.

"I'll tell them nothing," he said coldly. "I've made my peace with Robert. I'd not have him go off to war fearing that I'd inform our father of his shameful conduct. If Father were to hear of it, he'd not hesitate to cut Robert off without a penny! I'd not have that happen. I prefer to believe that Robert is, as he swears to me, truly in love with you, and, being of a passionate nature, was unable to restrain himself."

"'Tis no more than the truth!" Damaris cried. "And I'll not forgive you—not ever—for coming between us. I hate you. I shall hate you all my life."

Suddenly he smiled. "I think you'll find hatred to be a most enervating emotion, my dear Damaris." Moving to the door, he added, "I think you'd best rise and have your abigail pack your bandboxes. I've ordered the coach for eleven. I wish you a pleasant journey." He left, closing the door softly behind him.

Damaris glared after him. She had lost all desire to weep. Her fury had burned away her tears. Between her teeth, she muttered, "The time will come when you'll regret your interference in our lives. If Robert's not here to make you pay for it, I shall! Just you wait and see, Giles Harwine!"

CHAPTER
One

HEAT HUNG LIKE a pall over London. No vagrant breeze stirred the leaves on the trees lining the walks outside the Harwine town house. Damaris stood at the window in the second drawing room and pushed a damp curl out of her eyes. She longed for a snowstorm. Unfortunately, they occurred rarely in August.

"Ah, now that is something like. Turn around and let me see!"

Damaris whirled to find Lady Mary Gresham standing in the doorway, her green eyes glowing with approval. "That lavender is most becoming on you, my love," she continued. "And I am persuaded that the white lace ensemble you bought for evening wear will be even better. Lord, 'tis a relief to see you out of black. It made you look sadly sallow. How could you bear to face your

22

mirror these fifteen months past. I know how much you loved poor Robert, but you were not his widow. I am Francis' widow, but I could scarce wait to put on colors and I shall be even happier when I am entirely out of mourning. White, lavender and gray are well enough, but green is my shade. And I do think you should have purchased that golden silk that Madame Hortense showed you."

As Mary paused for breath, Damaris said reprovingly, "I could not wear yellow yet."

"I would if I were in your place," Mary said enviously. "And I did grieve for poor Francis—such a dreadful place to die, in the wilds of Canada—but I am sure he would not have wanted me to go about in black like a dowd. And he did die, Damaris. Robert is only reported missing in action, which is definitely not the same thing. If Francis had been merely reported missing, I should never have donned widow's weeds—not until I was completely sure."

"I know Robert is dead," Damaris said. "'Tis a feeling I have here." She put a hand to her heart.

Mary sighed. "I expect I agree. I cannot think that dearest Robbie would remain away from London, er . . . and you, my sweet, for this length of time." She glanced out of the window. "Look, you can see the flags in the parks. Which reminds me, I must find Giles." She drifted out of the room.

Damaris sent a hot look after her. She had been sorely tempted to give Mary a set-down for suggesting that the pleasures of the city exercised a greater hold over Robert than herself, but of course she dared not chide Mary. The young woman had invented a plan that would remove her from an environment she found galling, horrid, hateful, and demeaning. Indeed, any opprobrious adjective would suffice to describe her situation.

Damaris was thinking about Giles—or, more correctly now, Lord Harwine, Viscount Croy, the title he had inherited at his father's death. This sad event had taken place a scant three and a half weeks after Robert's departure for Canada. As had been feared, Lady Harwine had not long survived her husband. She had been in her grave less than a month when they received the news that Robert was missing, and, judging from the accounts of comrades-in-arms, presumed dead. It had been a terrible time for Deborah, Mary, Giles, and herself.

Thinking about it now, Damaris could still feel tears start to her eyes for what she considered a *quadruple* tragedy. Not only had she lost all whom she held dear, she had also been placed in the most untenable, the most unthinkable position! The man whose untimely intervention had kept her from enjoying the last hours she would ever spend on this earth with the man she loved was now her guardian!

"But it cannot be . . . 'tis unthinkable," she had wailed when given this information by a sober-faced and tight-lipped Giles.

"I am quite in agreement with you, Damaris. But unthinkable or not, it has been so set down in my father's will."

"But *my* father cannot have meant you to be my guardian!" she had expostulated.

"I am sure he did not, since I was but eleven when he died. However, much as I argued against it, 'twas the opinion of my father that I occupy that position until you have reached what your parent chose to deem the 'age of discretion.'"

"Three more years?" she had moaned.

A horror, still undiminished by the passage of time, arose in her mind as she remembered his answer. "Longer, I fear."

"Longer? But twenty-one is considered—"

"Sir Romulus Vardon thought differently. Twenty-five is the age stipulated in his will."

"But that is ridiculous!" she had cried.

"I am in total agreement. Unfortunately, it is too late to argue that point. Still, there is a clause that could shorten that span."

"And what is that?"

"If at any time before you reach your twenty-fifth birthday, you are wed to one who meets with your guardian's approval, naturally his—er my tenure will be at an end."

"But . . . but . . ." Damaris had wrung her hands. "I shall never marry. My heart is dead."

Giles had been looking very grim, but, to her surprise and subsequent ire, a gleam of laughter had flickered briefly in his green eyes. "We'll see how long you remain in that—er—debilitating condition, my dear Damaris."

Damaris glanced down at her lavender gown and flushed with annoyance. Though she hardly cared to admit it, even to herself, much of her reluctance to lay aside her somber garments stemmed from an effort to convince Giles that she had meant every word she had uttered. She must assure him that it was the weather— hot even for August—that had occasioned her decision, rather than any change of heart. "And," she muttered to herself, "if he makes any of his horrid caustic remarks on the subject, I'll remind him that this, too, is a mourning color!"

She sighed, wishing that Giles were not in residence. During the past two years, he had been much away on matters having to do with the supervision of his estates, or so he had said. Mary was sure that his frequent absences suggested that he had a mistress tucked away somewhere. Be that as it may, Damaris had not suffered under the yoke of his guardianship as much as she had feared. However, when he was at home, he had not spared her his opinion on her prolonged mourning, and during the last few months his comments on that subject had grown ever more trenchant. Indeed, at one point when she had purchased a bonnet with a drawstring which had brought two sections of a thick black veil together over her face, he had burst into unseemly laughter, saying with a dryness that had made her long to hit him, "Doing it a bit too brown, aren't you, my dear?"

With some difficulty, Damaris had swallowed a sharp retort and substituted a mournful "If you could see into my heart, Giles, you'd not say that."

"If I could see into your heart, Damaris, I should get a most fascinating look at your auricles and ventricles, but since that could take place only upon dissection, I am glad to be denied that privilege."

Damaris had longed to hurl her heavy straw bonnet into his smiling face but truthfully, after the novelty of the drawstring had passed, she had not worn it, mainly because it was a most unbecoming shape and the veil of such thickness as to distort her vision. She ground her teeth. The bonnet's disappearance had not gone unremarked.

"And what, pray tell, has happened to that—er theatrical addition to your wardrobe, my dear?" her tormentor had inquired.

"Theatrical addition?" she had questioned unwisely.

"Your curtained headpiece. I rather liked it."

"Indeed? I had the distinct impression that you did not."

"On the contrary, I found it very pleasant when the performance began and your face made its appearance."

These and other so-called witticisms had driven Damaris to say to Mary that if she had to spend even the smallest portion of the next five years in his company, she would need to remove to Bedlam!

"I quite understand," Mary had told her. "Though I expect it was kind of him to let me stay here at home, I have always found my brother a most oppressive presence. He is forever sure that he is right. But, my love, I believe I have a solution to both our problems."

"And what would that be?" Damaris had inquired breathlessly.

"I have it in mind to set up my own establishment in town. There is the most delightful house in Park Place which I can hire for a mere pittance, but of course I'd not dream of dwelling there without a female companion. And who better than yourself, dearest Damaris?"

"Oh!" Damaris had brought her hands together in what would have been a burst of clapping. Fortunately, she had remembered that such a display would have been quite unseemly in one given over to grief. Consequently, she had clasped them instead, but she had been quite unable to keep from remarking, though with restrained enthusiasm, "It is the most splendid notion!"

"Is it not?" Mary had smiled. "It was what I'd hoped to persuade poor, dear Francis to do."

"But did he not have a house in Marylebone Street?"

Mary had rolled her eyes. "Of a truth, he did. Or rather, his family did, and half the time the lot of 'em were in residence. My dear, such a pack of dowds as you never saw! Furthermore, once I'd married Francis, I found he cherished the warmest feelings for his estate outside of Lauceston, Cornwall—which, as you know, is the very end of nowhere. If I had known before we wed that . . . but no matter. I can only tell you that I shall never again make the mistake of loving anyone who does not reside a comfortable distance from town."

That conversation had taken place last week. Since then, she and Mary had spoken of little else. Under the guise of walking in the Park, they had visited the house and had gone as far as talking terms with Mr. Grimsby, its agent. Damaris was fully in agreement with Mary concerning its possibilities. Though it was but half the size of the Harwine town house, it had the virtue of being without both Giles and the unhappy memories of the rooms at home.

All too often, Damaris would come into the back

parlor or the library or one of the suites on the second floor and think of Lady Harwine at her needlepoint or Lord Harwine deep in a book. Of course, Robert's image was everywhere—on the stairs, outside her window flinging pebbles at the glass as he had that night he had returned from Spain. Or she remembered when they were younger and he teased her by popping out of some cupboard or from under a table. Certainly, it would be a blessing not to be pursued by those ghosts of a happier past. On the other hand, there were times when she wondered how she would feel being removed totally from a place where, save for her sojourns in the country, she had spent so much of her life? Still, if one part of her were uncertain about leaving, the other part would remind her again that this new domicile would not contain Giles Harwine. That one fact served to erase any qualms she might feel.

Giles himself provoked other memories—not only of his unwarranted interference that last night, but also of something else she could not forget. It came back to her at odd moments and never failed to send the color rushing to her cheeks. She saw Robert grabbing the poker and advancing purposefully upon his fallen brother while she, in an attempt to forestall what she feared might be murder, had thrown herself against Giles. Though she could not regret her timely intervention, she could not forget that she had been naked! Had Giles noticed? She could hope only that the exigencies of the moment had prevented that realization. Still, it was a most unwelcome and embarrassing recollection.

"I must get away," she murmured and then started as Mary came back into the room wearing a bonnet that framed her heart-shaped face becomingly and did not hide her bronze locks.

"You're going out?" Damaris asked.

"No, I mean yes. Guess what? No, do not guess, I

shall tell you." Mary smiled. "Giles has consented. Oh, I never, never thought he would."

"Really?" Damaris stared at her, wide-eyed.

"Honest and truly. And what is even more wonderful, he expressed a wish to accompany us. In fact, his consent hangs upon that, as I thought it might, but I do hope you'll not mind."

"To—to accompany us?" Damaris faltered. "I do not understand."

"My dear, do not look so distressed. I know 'tis a shock but certainly he'll furnish some protection, and there will be such a crush of cits to view the sea battle."

"The sea battle?"

"Yes, you must remember I mentioned it yesterday. 'Twill be on the Serpentine this afternoon—the British versus the Yankees and the French." She clasped her hands. "It should prove vastly entertaining."

"Oh, for the Jubilee," Damaris said weakly. "No, I had not forgotten but . . ." Suddenly she started to laugh.

"Dearest, what's amiss?"

Damaris lifted a flushed face. "I thought you meant that Giles had given his consent about the house. You did say you'd be asking him about it soon."

"Oh, the house." Mary laughed, too. "No, I haven't yet, but I am sure there'll be no trouble in obtaining his permission. Indeed, I thought it would be far more difficult to persuade him to this. He does loathe crowds. But 'tis not every day that we celebrate peace and the downfall of that monster, Napoleon."

"No, not every day," Damaris agreed and refrained from expressing her heartfelt wish that the celebrations could have taken place two years previously, before Robert had been posted to America. Still, perhaps it would not have made any difference since that conflict had been a thing apart, and, contrary to Lord Harwine's estimation, not ended yet. She sighed.

"Do not look so wistful, Damaris," Mary begged. "I know you long to be away from here, as I do, myself, and we soon shall be. I am convinced of it."

"Are you?" Damaris regarded her dubiously.

"Oh, yes, I am certain that Giles can have no objections to the plan. I am sure he finds the situation as odious as you do."

"Odious?" Damaris repeated thoughtfully. "Is that how he's described it to you?"

"Not in so many words. He's always been close-mouthed with me, but looks can speak volumes, can they not? I could always ascertain poor dear Francis' state of mind from the looks he directed at me. Such a bear as he could be on occasion—completely unreasonable— but that is aside from the point. Of course, due to our father's illness, Giles is used to undertaking unpleasant chores. Still, it cannot have been to his liking to be burdened with a female as melancholic and hostile as yourself."

Damaris bridled. "I have done my utmost in his presence to keep my melancholia to myself!" she exclaimed. "Has he told you I've been hostile?"

Mary shrugged. "I have just explained that Giles does not make me his confidante. I have merely assumed that, since you do not have a particularly good opinion of him, or he of you—"

"He has been speaking to you!" Damaris flared. "What has he said about me?"

"He hasn't said anything, dearest. Whatever is throwing you into your high-ropes?"

"You said he doesn't have a good opinion of me!"

"Oh, I really meant in general. I don't think Giles is fond of females. You know how serious-minded he is."

"Well," Damaris said coldly, "we haven't seen very much of each other in the past months. Until you came, there was your Cousin Phoebe to act as chaperone, and

I was much with her." Damaris grimaced at this particular recollection but forebore to comment on Phoebe Haverstoke's reign, now fortunately in the past. "Giles was generally away. On the few occasions he was here, we were wont to play chess, which required all our concentration."

Somewhat to her surprise, Mary's words concerning her brother's opinions hurt, though why this should be, she did not quite understand. A moment later, Damaris assured herself that it was merely surprise at an antagonism he must have taken considerable pains to keep from her. Indeed, of late he had seemed more teasing than anything else. Yet, thinking back on it, Damaris did remember his reluctance at becoming her guardian. She tossed her head. Certainly it could not match her feelings at being his ward.

"If Giles holds me in such dislike," she went on, "there can be nothing to keep us from removing to Park Place at the earliest possible moment."

"Oh, yes, I am positive that it is a *fait accompli,*" Mary said bracingly. "There's another reason why Giles will be more than delighted to be free of you—his marriage."

"His . . . marriage?" Damaris repeated. "He's betrothed?"

"Not yet, but he's nearing thirty, and 'twill be his duty to wed and beget an heir. If he does not, the title will revert to Cousin Phoebe Haverstoke's brother Osgood, who is even more odious than she. I am sure Giles would not want that to happen. And I am also sure that any female for whom he offered would hardly care to stay in a house with someone as pretty as yourself, perpetual mourning or not."

"She'd not need to worry on that count," Damaris said. "From what you've told me, it is obvious that he dislikes me as much as I dislike him."

"I am sure that is true, dear. However, wives do tend to be horridly jealous. If you'd ever been one, you'd understand. So many gentlemen have the philosophy that a bird in the hand is never the equal of the two or three they may snare in the bush. But let's not dwell on this any longer. If we are to go to the Park, we must start soon, else we'll never get a place by the water."

Mary had left Giles in the library, to which they proceeded. As they approached the doors, a shiver of fear ran through Damaris, followed by amazement. There was certainly no reason why, after all this time, those shining panels should remind her of the night Robert had returned from Spain. She shook her head and followed Mary inside, only to experience a completely unexpected shock as Giles, whose gaze had been bent on some papers, glanced up. She was used to seeing him but, for a brief moment, looking into his green eyes, she seemed to see Robert instead. The sensation did not pass immediately because he smiled, and for once that expression was without its usual irony.

Rising, he said with real pleasure, "Damaris in lavender!"

"I thought you must approve it," Mary commented. "The color's becoming to her, is it not?"

"Most becoming," he agreed with alacrity. Coming around the desk, he lifted Damaris's hand to his lips and added, "Might I hope that dull grief has finally taken wing?"

Annoyance flashed through Damaris. As usual, he was teasing her, daring to make light of the grief that had blighted her life. She ceased to be confused by his resemblance to Robert. She needed to remember that it was only skin deep, yet it did explain the conflicting feelings activated by Mary's revelations concerning his state of mind. She would be very glad when she and Mary had removed to an establishment where he could be admitted by invitation only. She said coldly, "Whether I go in black or purple, Giles, my feelings remain unchanged."

"Indeed?" To her further annoyance, his eyes gleamed with mocking amusement. "I have always counted consistency among the virtues."

Mary had a quelling look for Damaris. "I have just been explaining that you will accompany us to the Park. I hope you are still of the same mind."

"Since I have just declared myself in favor of consistency, it is unlikely that I should be of a different mind in so short a time. Furthermore, whatever the reason, I must count myself privileged to escort two such blooming beauties."

"La, Brother, how gallant you are become," Mary tittered and sketched a small curtsy.

Finding herself the recipient of another of Giles's mocking glances, Damaris longed to plead a sick headache, but, recollecting that if she were to prove a spoilsport, their large scheme might suffer, she said coolly, "If we're going, I expect we'd best be gone."

"I could not have put it more succinctly." Giles bowed. "By all means, let us be off to the wars."

CHAPTER
Two

THE FETE KNOWN as the *Grand National Jubilee for the Centenary of the Illustrious Family of Brunswick to the Throne of this Kingdom as well as the Anniversary of the Battle of the Nile* had been anticipated eagerly for most of the summer.

A date for the Jubilee had been announced several times and then abandoned for one reason or another, much, it was said, to the disappointment of such distinguished visitors as the Emperor of Russia and the King of Prussia, as well as other illustrious Royals. However, thanks to official dawdling, they were all gone home by August 1, 1814, which date marked the opening of the festivities. Still, once the fete was set up, all cavils vanished, for certainly it promised to be exciting.

Hyde Park, Green Park, the Mall of St. James's Park,

and Constitution Hill were thrown open to the public. The lawn of St. James's Park and the lower part of Green Park, also known as Birdcage Walk, were restricted to those people whose dislike of crowds had moved them to buy half-guinea tickets. However, there was enough amusement for everyone. All of Hyde Park was given over to a gigantic fair, while in St. James's Park there were boat races on the canal, and, for the edification of the people, a Chinese bridge and pagoda had also been erected. In Green Park a mammoth Castle of Discord would turn into a Temple of Concord—this last being a fireworks display. There was to be a balloon ascension in front of Buckingham House, but the main attraction for many was the naumachia—a mock sea battle demonstrating the might of the British Navy over such puny foes as the American and French fleets. This event was scheduled for six in the evening, but those who wanted to get a good view of the proceedings came as early as three hours prior to the designated time.

However, it was not a matter of lining up on the banks of the river and waiting for the excitement to begin. There was plenty of diversion to be found in the booths, which since Sunday, had been rising in the vicinity. Round, square, triangular, and polygonal, they were decorated with the flags of all nations. And here, much to the amusement of various spectators, considerable ingenuity was exhibited. The ensigns that fluttered from poles or decorated doorways had seen service in widely different capacities. Some of them had been fashioned from dilapidated petticoats and pantaloons stitched together into a single leg. Some banners, glittering with the insignia of the Regent, bore every evidence of having been bedsheets.

In addition to the booths there were also Punch-and-Judy shows, and on specially constructed platforms Messrs. Scowton, Richardson and Gyngel's theater companies performed such favorites as *The Beggar's Opera*, *Romeo and Juliet*, and the *Spectre Bride*.

Damaris walked beside Mary and Giles, all but convinced that her state of mind would not allow the infiltration of such pleasures as were now on view. However, it was difficult to remain unmoved by the excitement. The parks did look pretty with all the trees festooned with different colored lamps and, on walking up a rise of ground, she could see the ships lined up in the Serpentine awaiting the commencement of the naumachia.

"Oh, look!" Mary suddenly cried, pointing.

Gazing in that direction, Damaris saw a tent that looked as if it had been fabricated from any odd piece of material its maker could find, while its "flag" was a pair of monstrous drawers, which could only have been the property of the immense man who stood in front of the entrance issuing a stentorian invitation to come and look at the "'orrid, great dragon wot come from the jungles o' Afriky 'n' 'ad swallered a man of the girth o' 'is Royal 'ighness, the Prince Regent, afore it were captured 'n' brought to these 'ere shores."

"Should you care to view yon ''orrid great dragon'?" Giles smiled down at Damaris.

"Oh, I should," she said excitedly and without thinking. Thought came an instant later and with it the reflection that a grieving lady should scarcely be going in to gawk at some exhibition that was probably nothing but sham. Unfortunately, by that time it was too late to protest. Mary had pronounced herself equally eager to see the monster, and Giles had put down the necessary fee.

It was dark inside the tent. A rough personage endeavored to make the viewers file in an orderly line around a huge glass container, by making rough replies and rude jests as well as grumbling considerably once they had obtained a look at the monster. Damaris pressed close to the cage and saw a large, somnolent snake which, though quite long, did not look as if it had the capacity to swallow more than the mouse that was cowering at the far end of the container.

"Oh," someone groaned from behind them, "'Tisnt nothin' more than a ruddy great snake."

"No, it's more than that," Giles said to Damaris's surprise. "It's a python, and they do have the capacity to swallow small pigs, though I don't know about the Prince Regent."

"'Ere," a man growled, "wot're you sayin' about the Prince?"

"Er," another chimed in, "looks to me as if that there buck be levelin' an insult at 'is 'ighness."

"Oh, dear, Giles," Mary murmured, "you shouldn't have said anything."

"What I did say," Giles responded in clear, penetrating tones, "was that the snake is a python. I was leveling no insults at His Royal Highness, for whom I have the liveliest esteem."

"An' oi say 'e were insultin' 'is Majesty." A heavy-set man moved forward to glare belligerently at Giles from under tufted eyebrows. "An' also say 'e'd better be 'andy wi' 'is fives or 'e's a-goin' to 'ave a facer wot'll send 'em sprawlin'."

"'Twasn't 'is Majesty," a thinner man corrected punctiliously. "'Is Majesty's still alive, even if 'e *is* off 'is noggin."

"Off 'is noggin'! 'E's a sight brainer'n 'is son," a third man observed.

"Ere!" The heavy set fellow turned his fiery gaze on the man. "You take that back."

"Be damned if I do."

"Come." Giles caught at Damaris's arm and placed his other hand on Mary's shoulder. "It's turned political. We'd best be—" He broke off, startled, as the container suddenly shook from the combined weight of the several persons who had slammed against it.

Gazing into the case, Damaris caught sight of the python's small beady eyes. It seemed to her that the huge snake was staring directly at her. "Oh!" She moved against Giles, feeling uncomfortably like the mouse, which had lost its balance and lay on its back, waving its tiny, helpless limbs feebly.

"Come," Giles repeated, quickly shepherding both ladies outside. As they emerged from the tent, the sounds of strife increased in volume. Since it seemed expedient to get away as quickly as possible, it was not until they had reached a large wooden platform some distance away that Giles stopped to catch his breath. He gave an anxious look at his companions. "Are you—"

He broke off as a deep contralto intoned from the platform in rather petulant accents, "'Tis the nightingale and not the lark . . ."

Looking quickly upwards, Damaris saw a plump, middle-aged lady in a very curly, very blond wig. She wore a tight shift that did nothing to conceal her ample curves and was bending over a weedy youth, who appeared more bored than ardent when answering his beloved's protests.

"It should not surprise me if she were to wake the household with her plaints," Giles murmured. "And that must put another ending entirely upon the tragedy."

Staring at that moderately enraptured couple, Damaris had a sudden vision of Juliet's necessarily ancient parents tottering into their daughter's chamber, and she had considerable difficulty in choking back her giggles. As she clung tightly to Giles's arm, she realized that it had developed a suspicious quiver. Darting a glance at him, she found that he, too, was laughing. She met his twinkling eyes and flung a hand over her mouth, vainly trying to adhere to Cousin Phoebe's oft-repeated strictures on Decorum. Though she finally managed to subdue her giggles, she could not help think that it was much easier to be decorous when dressed in black.

Wearing colored gowns made her feel very odd, much like herself at seventeen before she had decided she was madly in love with Robert. She and Robert and Mary had giggled a lot when they were younger. They had even laughed in church, often going through the most painful facial contortions to avoid being observed by Lord and Lady Harwine. Love, she realized, had put a definite damper on her spirits, and grief had quelled them utterly.

Strangely enough, she was feeling marvelously free of both emotions now. She did not understand how that had happened. There was much that she was finding puzzling this afternoon, and that included the fact that she was actually enjoying Giles's companionship. No, that was not quite true; she did know why she was enjoying it. He was different this afternoon. For once he had come down from the pedestal he had occupied even before his father's death. Rather than being the enemy, he was on a level with Mary and herself and, though he was close to the sober age of thirty, he seemed much younger. She tried to ascertain the reasons for the change. Was it a matter of attitude or appearance? Finally she concluded it was both.

Generally, Giles dressed very neatly, even severely. Without having the slightest pretensions toward dandyism, he did follow some of the dicta of Beau Brummel. His garments were well-cut and never ostentatious. He favored coats of superfine, generally in gray or, on special occasions, bottle-green. He preferred buckskin breeches, and his Hessians were always polished to a high shine. He disdained gold fobs, wearing leather instead, and there were no rings on his slender fingers. His shirts were always highly starched, but his cravats were never of a design so intricate that his valet was kept arranging them for hours. His hair, which was inclined to curl, was so rigorously pomaded that it was generally flat against his head—an effect which, Damaris suddenly realized, made him look older than his years. At present, his hair had fallen into deep and most becoming waves about his face. In deference to the heat, he had, with several apologies, removed his coat, draping it over his shoulders. He had also loosened his cravat and rolled up his sleeves. Somehow this unusual lack of satorial perfection made him much more approachable.

As she was making this inventory, Damaris looked up to find that Giles was visiting, in turn, a measuring glance upon her. Meeting his eyes, she discovered with a little jolt of surprise that for once she was not uncomfortably reminded of Robert. Indeed, there was something about his look that did not recall his brother at all. At first she was not sure what had made the difference, and then she knew. Each time their glances had locked, Robert had always been the first to turn away, but Giles did not turn away. His gaze was steady and even compelling. Indeed, it was *she* who felt the need to drop her eyes and who found her cheeks burning and her thoughts sadly scattered for reasons she did not understand.

Mary, bless her, created a most welcome diversion. "Goodness, Giles," she said, "look at all the people heading for the Serpentine. Do you not think 'tis time we joined them?"

Giles turned in the direction of the river. "Yes, they are queuing up." He stretched out his arms. "Please, you must hold on to me. There will be much jostling for position, and in unity there is strength. More to the point, we could easily be separated. I need not warn you of the difficulties that could be encountered by a lone female in so vast an assembly."

"Oh, come." Mary giggled. "I am sure everyone will be far more interested in the sea battle."

"You underestimate your charms, my dear Mary, as well as those of your companion."

"La." Mary favored him with an arch look. "I believe you're growing gallant, Giles—or perhaps 'tis merely practice?"

"Practice?" he inquired with a lift of an eyebrow.

"Certainly there must come a time when you'll need to solicit the hand of some female suitable to become Viscountess Croy."

To Damaris's regret, the laughter that had been lighting Giles's eyes fled suddenly. He visited a stern and even a forbidding look upon his sister as he said quellingly, "'Twill be a long time before that happens, I can assure you."

Mary remained undaunted. "Surely I cannot understand how you can wear the willow for nigh on eight years."

Giles did not answer her. He merely offered his arm, and Damaris, taking his other arm, found it tense. Glancing at his face, she saw a little muscle quivering in his cheek. She darted an angry look at Mary, wondering why she had seen fit to raise the specter of the unhappy Lady Laura on this pleasant afternoon. Yet at the same time she found it surprising that Giles remained so faithful to her memory. She was sure that, if Robert had been similarly bereft, the lady would have been forgotten before the grass had grown on her grave, he being much akin to Mary in temperament; and certainly she was not grieving overmuch for Francis! However, immediately this thought crossed her mind, Damaris was shocked at her lack of loyalty to her late love. If she had died and Robert had remained alive... But there was no time to reflect on that. She must needs keep up with Giles.

Despite the masses of people already crowding the banks of the Serpentine, Giles managed to find them a place near the water. As they waited for the entertainment to commence, he, coming out of the ill humor Mary's remark had occasioned, waxed most informative on the rows of ships anchored in those quiet waters. Indicating several frigates flying the Stars and Stripes, he explained that the American vessels would take part in the first engagement.

Further away floated six French vessels, including a lordly three-decker which was the admiral's ship. As Giles identified it, he was put in mind of the Battle of the Nile, in which the late Lord Nelson had routed the French fleet and left Napoleon's forces stranded in Egypt. Though he had been but thirteen at the time, he had evidently perused all the available accounts, and he described the encounter so vividly that Mary declared she could actually smell the smoke from the burning French flagship, *L'Orient*.

Giles laughed and then sobered. "I suppose I remember that so well because of poor little Giacomo Casabianca."

"And who was he, pray?" Mary demanded.

"He was a lad, younger, I think, than myself at the time, the son of the ship's commander. His father had ordered him to remain on deck, and when the father was mortally wounded, the boy stayed to tend his father rather than follow the rest of the crew into the lifeboats. They died together when the ship blew up. The explosion was heard fifteen miles away."

"Oh, dear, poor little boy!" Damaris turned away quickly and found the line of vessels turned blurry by her tears. But at that moment, the English fleet weighed anchor, and, catching a fine topgallant breeze from the west, came down on the Yankee vessels and fired a broadside at them. The sound of the cannons was realistic enough to make the watchers on shore gasp and put hands to their assaulted eardrums, keeping them there as the Americans returned fire. Then the English ship came close to the wind and passed under the stern of the Yankee frigate, ramming her as she went by. Then ranging on her starboard side, she delivered a second broadside. A desperate cannonade commenced, lasting fully three-quarters of an hour! A second English frigate joined the fray, and Damaris was shocked to see toppling masts and holes blown in the sides of all the participating ships. Eventually, and much to her relief, the battle ended with the English sailors clambering aboard the American frigate and exchanging the Stars and Stripes for the Union Jack to the accompaniment of a great roar from those on shore.

Caught up in the spirit of this heroic—if mock—victory, Damaris actually jumped up and down. "Oh, it is lovely to see them lose!" she shouted. As she turned to Giles, her eyes narrowed as a skinny lad reached a hand toward the watch attached to the fob at his waist. With a lightning movement, she slapped the boy's hand down, only to have her arm seized by a rough-looking man standing beside him. Twisting her arm painfully, he yelled, "Wot're ye doin' to me son?"

Immediately the boy dashed away, even as Damaris, unmindful of the throbbing pain in her arm, cried accusingly, "You're son's a thief."

"Damaris!" Giles had whirled.

"A thief, is 'e?" growled her captor and suddenly he went staggering back as Giles dealt him a sharp blow to the chin.

"Oo-er, that were a real facer," someone in the crowd said admiringly.

"Aye, got'm a nice pair o'fives, 'e 'as."

"Did he hurt you?" Giles demanded a trifle breathlessly.

"No . . . oh, look out!" Damaris shrieked as the rough man threw himself on Giles, pinioning his arms while another equally ill-favored rogue aimed an immense fist at his nose. Fortunately, Giles was able to twist his head away, but the blow slammed against the side of his mouth. His captor loosened his grip, and Giles dropped to the ground.

"Giles!" Damaris fell on her knees beside him.

"'Ere, wot's this?" a constable demanded, shouldering his way through the throng that had gathered around the fallen man.

"These men..." Damaris began and paused, staring about her in confusion. The pair of ruffians were nowhere to be seen, but a contingent of bystanders were eagerly telling the constable that they had gone in what appeared to be a dozen different directions.

"Wot 'appened, miss?" The constable leaned over Damaris.

"A lad tried to steal his watch. I caught him at it, and the man said he was his father..."

"Thieves." The constable sighed. "An' that's their lay."

"Aye," someone said behind them, "used a lad as their nipper, they did."

"Born to be 'anged, they was," remarked another interested observer.

"An' on a day o' national glory."

"Aye, 'tis a great shame...the shame o' the country."

Unmindful of the growing babble, Damaris sat down on the grass and eased Giles's head onto her lap. To her horror, his lip was cut badly, and a thin trickle of blood coursed down his chin.

"Is 'e 'urt bad, miss?" the constable demanded.

"No," Giles mumbled. "Loosened a tooth 'tis all."

"Oh, dear, what happened? I could not push through the crowds, I didn't know he'd left my side until—" Mary broke off with a shudder as she stared down at her brother. "I think I shall swoon," she said faintly.

Damaris glared at her. "If you do, I'll never forgive

you. Please dip your handkerchief in the water so that I may wash the wound. Hurry."

"Didn't none o' ye 'ave a good look at 'em?" The constable was moving among the bystanders.

Meanwhile as Mary went toward the water's edge, Damaris took a corner of her skirt to wipe the blood from Giles's chin.

"No," he protested weakly. ". . . too pretty . . . too pretty to stain." He stared up at her. "Tears . . ." he said. "Do not weep, Damaris. I am all right." He frowned, adding worriedly, "But you—are you in pain, my dear?"

"No, nothing happened to me."

"Your arm." His frown deepened. "I saw him twist it."

"'Twas nothing. Now you must lie still."

Drops of water splashed against her face as Mary held out a dripping handkerchief. "Here," she said unnecessarily.

"Ah, good." Taking it from her, Damaris daubed Giles's lips. "We must get him home."

Giles shook his head. "But I am quite all right," he assured her, speaking a little thickly. Lifting his head from her lap and pressing a hand to the ground, he managed to sit up. "I should like to see the British engage the French."

"You may read about it," Damaris told him. "I am sure that an imagination such as you have displayed will furnish as good an account of the action as you are like to see this day."

"You ought to go home," Mary agreed. "You don't look at all the thing, Giles."

He clambered to his feet and stood staring at Damaris, his bruised mouth twisted into a grin. "Which of us is the guardian, pray?" he demanded, extending a hand to her.

Without taking it, Damaris rose, saying severely, "On

this occasion, it seems that I must be."

Laughter brightened his eyes. "Very well. I shall recognize your authority, but do not imagine that I shall allow you to occupy that position permanently."

Damaris was conscious of considerable relief at his capitulation. "I do not think I should like it." She smiled.

"Ah." His stare was enigmatic. "We are in agreement at last."

CHAPTER
Three

MARY, DRESSED FOR WALKING, looked at Damaris with no little annoyance. "But you said you would accompany me..." She paused and looked toward the stairs. Lowering her voice, she finished, "to Park Place."

Damaris frowned. "Peake's been with Giles for the better part of an hour. I want to wait and see how he is."

"Lord, he can only be better," Mary said sharply. "He has had a full day to rest."

"Peake told me he had a bad headache."

"La, my dear, this is an about-face. Sure my brother has a hard enough head and will not die of a knock or two. Still, it cannot but please him to have you lingering about like a pet spaniel."

Damaris flushed. "I do not like your analogy, Mary,"

she returned crisply. "'Tis only natural that I'd be concerned since I am partly responsible for his condition."

"How so?" Mary said in astonishment. "You didn't set those ruffians on him."

"If it were not for my crying out..."

Mary threw up her hands. "You have an uncommon long reach, my love, if you will take that blame upon yourself. But no matter, I have an appointment with Mr. Grimsby and can tarry no longer." With an exasperated look, Mary left.

Damaris glanced up the stairs. It was all she could do not to beg the valet to let her care for his master. If Giles had been unconscious, she would have done just that. But, the headache notwithstanding, he was in possession of his senses and, when she had begged to nurse him, he had sent Peake back with an unequivocal refusal. Damaris gave a small, mirthless laugh. What she did not hesitate to describe as his overdeveloped sense of propriety kept him from letting a young, unmarried female into his bedroom. It did not matter that the said female had known him nearly all her life and that they had been raised as brother and sister. He must needs abide by principles ingrained in him from the cradle, or so it appeared.

It was amazing how different he was from Robert. A rueful smile touched the corners of Damaris's mouth. Though she found his strict moral code a little ridiculous, she could not help but admire him for maintaining his high principles when he might as easily have taken full advantage of their situation. Not all guardians were so circumspect. If Robert had been in his position, she would not have been denied admittance to his room. She flushed. She could hardly compare the motives of the two men. Robert had been in love with her and mad to possess her. Giles entertained no such feelings. If he had... She shook her head. If he had, his conduct would have remained unchanged. Giles was an honorable man. He had high standards, and, in consequence, he was depending upon his valet to nurse him.

She could have made him much more comfortable, that she knew. She could have prepared herb teas, rubbed his head with cologne, and read to him. She could also have thanked him for his intervention in her behalf more promptly than had been possible. She was conscious, too, of feelings that went deeper than mere gratitude. Before the altercation with the thieves, she had been enjoying his companionship, and, despite what Mary had said earlier in the day, it seemed to her that he had been finding a similar pleasure in her society—and why was she dwelling on that? Really, her thoughts were going off in all directions! He . . . She tensed. She had heard a door open and footsteps coming along the upper hall from the direction of Giles's chamber.

"Peake!" she called, starting up the stairs. "How is he?"

"He is feeling much better, thank you."

With a little squeak of surprise, Damaris was about to run up the stairs, but this intention was forestalled by Giles, who had already started down.

"Why are you out of bed?" she demanded sternly.

"I have told you," he replied equably.

Damaris waited for him in the hall. "You are looking very pale," she observed with concern. "You oughtn't to be up yet. Your head—"

"Is harder than you might think," he returned, echoing Mary. "I do not believe I have thanked you sufficiently for that brave—if foolhardy—rescue of a watch I treasure since it was given me by my father, who received it from his father."

"I wish you'd not been so hurt," she replied, looking at his mouth, which, while less swollen, was still puffy and discolored. "And your bruises were sustained on my behalf, so it is I who must thank you."

"We shall ladle great heaps of gratitude upon each other." He smiled. "But your arm." He looked anxious. "Is it still stiff?"

"Not in the least," Damaris lied, hoping he had not noticed that she had been holding it a trifle awkwardly.

However, he must have noticed for he said with a little laugh, "We're a proper pair of invalids, are we not, my dear?" He ran a hand down her arm gently, his eyes full of a remembered anger. "I wish I'd been able to avenge you properly."

As gentle as his touch had been, it left odd sensations in its wake. Damaris said rather breathlessly, "You avenged me very properly indeed, Giles."

He flushed, "I should have preferred to do much more, my dear. And I must not forget to convey Dr. Beauchamp's thanks to you, as well as my own, for those compresses which much reduced the swelling of my mouth. Though it's still not a pretty sight, he tells me 'twill heal the faster because of your ministrations. And that is all to the good, for I am due to drive to the country tomorrow and must needs meet with Mrs. Lidgate. And you know that she is a great one for fussing over the lot of us, as if she were yet our nurse."

Damaris was aware of burgeoning regret. "You're not going to the country so soon!"

"I must. As usual, there are problems which I left unresolved on my last visit."

"But surely 'twould be better were you to wait another day," she said anxiously. "You are scarcely well enough to attempt so long a journey."

"I am sure I shall be tomorrow—and my estate agent is expecting me."

"Oh, dear!" Damaris cried impulsively. "I wish I could help you."

A whimsical smile twisted a corner of his mouth.

"Now that I consider a very noble suggestion."

"Noble?"

"Knowing your great distaste for the country."

Damaris blushed and said defensively, "No one could enjoy the country with Cousin Phoebe about." She looked at him apprehensively, remembering belatedly that the chaperonage of Cousin Phoebe had been his idea.

Much to her relief, Giles merely chuckled and said, "Well, at least that affliction is at an end." He stared at her for another moment. "You have changed since those days, my dear."

Meeting his eyes, Damaris said in a low voice, "Do you really think so?"

He nodded. "I always try to speak the truth." He added almost abruptly, "I must do some work in the library." He paused then added, "I almost forgot to tell you. I want you to let me replace your purple gown."

"You don't need to replace it," she said quickly.

"But I must. 'Twas my blood spotted it."

Damaris had an instant and painful vision of Giles lying with his head on her lap, weakly protesting the staining of that same gown. She looked down, saying softly, "Surely I'd not hold you to blame for that."

"I should like you to have another like it. 'Twas most becoming."

"I . . . thank you. I shall order one then."

"And others besides, I hope. In colors."

"I've done with mourning, Giles," she said on a breath.

"I am delighted to hear it, my dear." He smiled. "And now off to work." He went down the passageway toward the library.

Watching him, Damaris felt oddly lonely and, blinking, she found that there were tears in her eyes.

Damaris felt warm, and her feet were tired. Mary had brought her to the house in Park Place and, though they had pointed out that they needed to be home early so that they might rest for the ball that night, Mr. Grimsby had led them on far too extensive a tour of the upper floor. They were now in the front bedroom and Mary, casting a critical look at its two small windows, said, "I cannot think this chamber very commodious."

"True." Mr. Grimsby fiddled with one of his fobs and added nervously, "But there is the Park—an exceptional view, milady."

"Miss Vardon will scarcely have room for her abigail." Mary frowned.

Damaris bit down a wry smile. Despite the fact that she would share half the expenses of the house, Mary had naturally assumed that she would have the smaller of the two front rooms. However, Damaris was quick to remember, without Mary's presence, she must remain at home—or rather, in that mansion which she had been accustomed to describe as her home. Very recently it had been proven that, despite her seventeen years in one or another of the Harwine establishments, she had no real ties to the family.

Damaris might look on Mary as a sister and on Giles as an older brother—she shook her head vigorously, rejecting even a courtesy relationship with *him*. She did not regard Giles as family. She never had. Until recently he had been the enemy. And now... She would have run her hands through her hair had she not remembered in time that she was wearing a delicate bonnet that would not take well to this outward manifestation of her pain and anger.

"Love," Mary said, "Mr. Grimsby thinks we ought to have a quick look at the third-floor rooms where the servants will sleep. Will you come?"

"No," Damaris said hastily, "I think I should leave those arrangements to you. I would rather go back to the drawing room. I find it passing warm up here."

"It is." Mary had a stern look for little Mr. Grimsby.

"'Tis a pity the house is so situated that there is little in the way of cross-ventilation."

"But milady, it is so felicitously located," the agent said persuasively.

"Oh, yes, I'm not disputing that," Mary assured him as they passed out of the room.

Hurrying down the stairs, Damaris came into the drawing room. It, too, was small and, at present, far from prepossessing. It had been hung with flowered paper of an appalling pink, now faded in spots and marked with squares and circles that indicated spots where pictures and possibly mirrors had hung. A heavy coating of dust covered the marble mantelpiece and dust balls littered the floor. Judging by the thickness of the cobwebs clinging to the corners of the ceiling and to the dusty chandelier, Mr. Grimsby must have had this particular property on his hands for quite a while, felicitous location or no. That, of course, might have been due to its lack of space. But it would do very well for herself and Mary and, if it had been possible, she would have been more than content to have moved in this very day!

Crossing to one of the front windows, Damaris sat down on its wide sill. In common with its counterpart upstairs, it commanded an excellent view of the Park, and, seeing those green vistas shimmering in the hot noon sun, she was unwillingly reminded of Giles and her purple gown. His insistence upon replacing it, coupled with his mood on the morning he had left for the country, had given rise to considerable thinking and, though she hated to admit it even to herself, hoping. As a result, she had bundled up all her black garments and presented them to Sara. Her abigail had looked less than pleased by this gesture. "I expect I'll gi' 'em to my aunts—one o' 'em's sure to die eventually, Miss Damaris, and of course them bein' older, they must 'ave friends wot'll be doin' it one o' these days." The girl had brightened considerably when Damaris had subsequently commenced visiting various mantua makers. Probably the little minx thought she was due for hand-me-downs, but she must wait, for nearly everything in Damaris's wardrobe was new. In addition to the lavender gown, she had ordered several more dresses in shades which were not even half-mourning. She was currently wearing one of them, a bright yellow Indian chintz high dress. She had also purchased the golden silk Mary had admired and a round gown in shot silk that looked pink one moment and purple the next. Also swelling her armoire were a French gauze afternoon dress in white with the new shorter waist and a charming rose gown with matching pelisse for cool fall mornings. The chintz had been ready a week ago, but she had put it on fresh this morning because Giles had returned from the country late last night.

"Hah!" Damaris spoke aloud and so explosively that her tones seemed to bounce off the walls. She put a hand over her mouth and prayed she had not been overheard. If she had been, she would tell them she had seen a mouse. After a moment, she put the mouse to rest and reluctantly fixed her mind on the sad events of the morning. Though she had expected to meet Giles at breakfast, she had been informed by the housekeeper that he had gone early to the library.

Damaris had partaken of chocolate and a croissant. Then pronouncing herself tolerably well-filled, she had ignored eggs, roast beef, neat's tongue and broiled tomatoes in favor what she had described to the maid as "food for the mind"—a book. Her coming into the library had a direct bearing on the reasons why she was sitting on the windowsill of this dim, dusty, dreary, and depressing mansion.

Unwillingly, she envisioned the scene in the library. She had found Giles studying some sheets of figures. He had looked up quickly with a warm smile. "Good morning, Damaris."

"Good morning," she returned, feeling unaccountably self-conscious. "I . . . had breakfast and thought I would read, but if I am interrupting you . . ."

"'Tis no matter. It is a most welcome interruption. Is that not a new gown you are wearing?"

"One of several, and none black," she said pointedly, wondering if he remembered what *he* had said to her before leaving for the country.

If he had, he made no mention of it. He said merely, "Very good, my dear. You are far too young to go about in garb that best becomes a raven. I hope this change in attire betokens other even more important changes," he added meaningfully.

Damaris had been conscious of a peculiar upheaval in the region of her solar plexus. However, she had said calmly enough, "I have told you that I am done with mourning."

"Yes, I remember that, and I am glad you are still of the same mind." He pointed to a chair. "Do sit down. I have had it in mind to speak to you, and this is as good a time as any."

There was an appraising look in his eye which she had been hard put to interpret, but which had made her heart beat faster. At that moment, she had discovered that her senses were much scattered. She hoped she would not have difficulty concentrating on whatever he had to tell her. A bitter sound escaped her, one that never could have been mistaken for a laugh as she now recollected that she had had no difficulty following his miserable meaning!

Damaris had sat down in a side chair with carved arms ending in snarling lion's heads. As a child, she had called it her throne. She winced. So many memories were bound up with that house, which she intended to leave—as soon as possible!

Reluctantly, she turned her mind on Giles. He had

leaned forward, and she had seen that his mouth bore no trace of the battering he had received. She was relieved. She would not have wanted any of his features to be marred. He was really a very handsome man and, unless her memory were playing her tricks, she no longer found so marked a resemblance between him and his brother. Of the two, Giles definitely had the stronger countenance. There was determination in the set of mouth and chin—but why was she thinking of such things, she wondered.

In that moment, her feelings had crystalized! All at once she had realized that she was extremely attracted to him! This revelation had been followed immediately by speculation. What did he feel about her? And what did he want to tell her? Certainly he was regarding her very intently. Why?

In that moment he said, "You are young, my dear. Not yet twenty..." Was there a touch of regret to his tone? Was he remembering the nine years between them? Nine, yes, but no more than nine, in fact less—eight years and nine months.

"I am twenty," she said quickly. "My birthday was in March—when you were in the country."

"Twenty, is it?" He sounded surprised. "Well, that's not a great age, but certainly it's time you started going to balls and routs. You must remember that you are eminently eligible."

"Eligible?" Damaris repeated, confused.

"You are an heiress, my dear. And, from all indications, it would seem you are past your first grief. It is not meant that a young and lovely woman such as yourself should remain attached to the past. 'Tis time you were wed."

"Wed?" Her heart gave a great throb. "Wed!" she exclaimed.

Giles nodded, adding gravely, "I have long wanted

to bring this matter to your attention, and now that—"

"But I could not!" she cried.

Giles looked surprised and a little disappointed. "You cannot mean to remain a spinster, my dear Damaris."

She rose. "I could not c-consider marriage," she cried hotly. "I just couldn't."

His look was quizzical. "Very well, child, I shan't press you. But I do hope you'll be of a different mind soon. I am convinced that you were never meant to practice good works or collect cats—or—er, small spaniels."

"Cats or small spaniels?" she echoed, bemused.

His whimsical smile, her favorite of all his expressions, appeared. "Many maiden ladies do. Or they embroider altarcloths for deserving clerics. I cannot see you resigning yourself knowingly to so mundane an existence."

Of course he was teasing, but it made her very angry—more than angry. With a return of all her previous animosity, Damaris said defiantly, "My heart remains in Robert's grave."

Giles gave her a long, measuring look. "Do you know, Damaris, I am not sure I believe you. Furthermore, I am not even sure you believe it yourself."

"Believe as you wish," she returned curtly. "However, though you occupy the position of my guardian, you'll not force me into marriage!" Turning on her heel, she quitted the room abruptly, giving the door a bang that raised a series of echoes down the hall and caused old Travers, the butler, who was passing at that moment, to regard her with amazement.

Upon reaching her own chamber, Damaris gave full vent to her fury, drumming her feet on the floor and heaving a book through the open window with a force that sent it flying over the fence. She did regret that particular demonstration of anger, for it had been a first edition of *Childe Harold's Pilgrimage* signed by its author, the poet Byron. After calming down, she went to search for it, but did not find it.

Now, sitting on the windowsill and remembering her loss and reasons for it, her fury rose to the point where she wished she had something else to hurl, something that would hit the opposite wall and shatter. For she had just realized the total import of what Giles had been saying.

It stemmed from that day in the park when she had jokingly appointed herself Giles's guardian in order to coax him home. Afterward, she had averred that she would not like to keep that position permanently, and Giles had blurted out, "We are in agreement at last."

And what did that mean?

It meant that he wanted to be relieved of his responsibilities. That was what really lay behind all his talk of her marriage! It must also explain his frequent absences from home. Probably there was a female lurking in the country and, as Mary had suggested, he considered his ward an encumbrance! Well, she would be an encumbrance no longer! She glared at a spot that must once have been occupied by a huge portrait. Mentally, she filled it with the likeness of her reluctant guardian. He must be very reluctant indeed; straining at the bit, in fact.

"Oh," she muttered, "if only I could move in here tonight. I'd not mind the dust or the small space or anything." Of course, there still remained the matter of Giles's consent. She could not imagine him refusing. Most likely he would dance for joy at the very notion. She had half a mind to tell him about it tonight at Almack's. She glared at another spot—a small round one which may have been occupied by a convex mirror. It was a pity the object had been removed. Hurled against the opposite wall, it would have made a most satisfying crash—and brought her seven years of bad luck to add to twenty of the same.

Probably the reason they were going to one of Almack's Wednesday Night Subscription Balls was because Giles was planning to get her married as soon as possible. No doubt he would bestow her hand upon the first gallant who asked for a dance. She never should have consented to attend it. But it had been at Mary's earnest request that she had capitulated.

"For though I'll not be dancing, my love, and must be present only as your chaperone since I am not completely out of mourning, it would be so pleasant to be where there is music and laughter."

Notwithstanding this wistful prompting, a refusal had yet trembled on Damaris's tongue. Then she had reminded herself that she might be able to dance with Giles, and she had capitulated.

"But," she whispered now, "I'll refuse every partner who offers for me and that should convey something to the noble Viscount Croy!

Alas, for all her resolutions. Damaris had reckoned without the waltz.

Though much favored by the Prince Regent, this dance had been very slow to invade the sacred precincts of Almack's. Lady Jersey and the other six patronesses of those exclusive Assembly Rooms had found it far too daring until Princess Lieven, the beautiful wife of the Russian ambassador, had gone defiantly through its paces with Lord Palmerston. After that, no less a personage than the Emperor of Russia had followed suit with the result that the whole of the *ton* was now afflicted with "waltz mania."

At Mary's urging, Damaris had practiced the waltz with her. They had pushed back the furniture in the second parlor and whirled around the room to the sound of Mary's voice counting out the rhythms of three-quarter time. Yet, though Damaris had learned the steps, she had had no real conception of how the dance would appear when performed by stylishly garbed couples on the mirror-bright floors of the ballroom.

One of the popular German waltzes imported by the Regent had just been announced when Mary, Damaris, and Giles arrived. As the musicians struck up the tune, Damaris found its measures most compelling. Despite her resolution to remain with Mary in those spindly chairs set aside for dowagers, chaperones, and some of their unfortunate charges, she felt herself beguiled by the siren melody.

"Oh, dear," Mary moaned, "listen to that waltz!"

A side glance at her companion assured Damaris that laughter and music would not suffice for poor Mary. Her foot was tapping and her body, sheathed in white lace, seemed about to carry her onto the floor, conventions or not!

At that moment, Giles, to whom Damaris had not addressed a single word that evening, came to stand beside her. In spite of her resentment, it was impossible not to admit that he looked very handsome in his black satin evening attire. In fact, as far as she could see, none of the gentlemen in her immediate vision were half so attractive. That her opinion was shared by a number of other females was also obvious. Indeed, it seemed to her that Giles was the recipient of many languishing glances. Consequently, it could only please her that his appreciative green gaze was fixed on her. Or perhaps he was admiring her gown. No, though she was not vain, she knew that the golden silk with its floss trim at neckline and skirt was particularly becoming. The color flattered her complexion and, as the mantua maker insisted, only a female with her slim shape could appear to advantage in such a hue. She was wearing her mother's topaz tiara, necklace, and bracelets, and the effect of these had moved Sara to remark, "Oh, miss, you won't be a-sittin' down this evening."

Hard on this particular memory, Giles said, "Might I hope that you will favor me with this waltz, Damaris?"

"Oh," she breathed, "I should be delighted." She blushed. She had not meant to appear so eager, but, she assured herself fiercely, her acquiescence had nothing to do with her partner. If the devil himself had asked her for a dance, she would not have been able to resist the temptation of joining those whirling couples. That did not mean she forgave Giles. Her anger was burning as brightly as ever and would remain in abeyance only until the music ended. She tried not to appear too excited as Giles led her onto the floor.

He danced beautifully. He was wonderfully light on his feet. Damaris was aware of an excitement inside her that had nothing to do with the music. She also realized why the waltz had been thought so daring. It was certainly a new and heady experience to be partnered by only one man rather than seeing him ever so often as they moved through the complicated turns of a quadrille or country dance. Though she and Giles danced at arm's length and his hold on her was very light, they had perforce to stare into each other's faces.

She did not think she had ever seen him looking quite so handsome. He had such beautiful eyes—a translucent green. Amazingly, she had never noticed the length of his lashes or the fact that they actually had a slight curl to them. Once more it was borne in on her that he was exceptionally well-built—so broad a chest, so slim a waist—and he did not need padding to make his legs appear at their best in white silk stockings. A vagrant wish that they need not have danced so far apart arose in her mind. It would have been much more exciting to be held closer, very close, close enough so that she might feel the beating of his heart, so that his arms might tighten and, instead of dancing, they would be standing still, caught in a crushing embrace.

Damaris stifled a giggle. These were hardly the sentiments that should be going through the head of a well-brought-up young female. They were even less appropriate when she remembered that she was dancing with a gentleman who was more than eager to consign one to the first man who offered for her.

"You are uncommonly graceful, my dear," Giles murmured.

Without thinking, Damaris replied, "I have an uncommonly graceful partner." She blushed again. She had spoken only the truth, but it sounded as if she were flirting with him, which she most definitely was not.

"You are kind to say so." He smiled. "I've not had much experience at this sort of thing."

"I cannot believe that," Damaris returned and was once more embarrassed. Again she had spoken truly. Again it had come out sounding provocative. "I mean ..." she added and was forced to stop conversing because he had whirled her about in a turn so complicated that it gave the lie to his assertions. She wondered where he had learned to dance so beautifully and with whom. It could not have been with the late Lady Laura, because the waltz had not been in fashion six years ago. Did he still mourn his lost love? She could not believe that. Lady Laura was an old ghost now, and Robert was another. The living should not be intimidated by the dead. With a sense of real regret, Damaris realized that the music was drawing to a close.

Judging from Giles's expression, he, too, cherished regrets that the waltz had ended. A quadrille had been announced, and Damaris hoped he would ask her to be his partner, but he did not.

However, as he accompanied her from the floor, she was pleased to find herself surrounded by several other gentlemen. Unlike Giles, they were all extremely eager to dance with her. If she would have traded all their flattering invitations for another waltz with Giles, he would not know that. Nor would he have an opportunity to ask her again, even if he were so minded. Let him see that she was not dependent upon his good graces or cast down by the lack of them, Damaris thought defiantly, as she promised one gentleman the present quadrille, another a waltz, and a third a country dance. In an amazingly short time, the spokes of her little ivory fan were completely inscribed.

Later, returning to the floor with a tall youth whose name she had not even heard, Damaris tried to catch a glimpse of Giles, whom she had not seen for at least an hour. Finally she did see him. He was in earnest conversation with a tall woman in white lace. Was he asking her to dance, she wondered jealously? Damaris's partner was escorting her toward a group of dancers lined up for a country dance. Still, she managed to direct another glance over her shoulder and with some amusement realized that the woman in white lace was Mary. She was now sitting down in one of the chairs along the far wall and glaring at Giles. Not far away, a lone gentleman watched, an expression of mingled regret and wry laughter on his face. Damaris guessed that he must have asked Mary for a dance and that her brother had reminded her that she was a comparatively recent widow. Damaris grimaced, wondering if there were ever a time when he did not do obeisance to the dictates of Polite Society.

"Miss Vardon," her partner said edgily, "the dance is about to begin."

Seeing that he was looking a trifle cast down, Damaris quickly favored him with a ravishing smile. "Is it? Oh, I do love a country dance." It was amazingly pleasant to see how quickly his good humor was restored. It was also very flattering to one whose self-esteem was still much in need of bolstering. Indeed, an hour later, when Giles emerged from the card room to signal that they must leave, she was quite disappointed.

"Well," Mary observed, as they were putting on their cloaks, "you had a notable success."

"I did, didn't I?" Damaris said artlessly, and she executed a little waltz step. "It was so lovely, and so very many gentlemen..." Meeting Mary's resentful stare, Damaris broke off quickly, adding, "I do wish you might have joined in the dancing." The moment she had spoken, she regretted those words. She had forgotten the little incident by the chairs. "I mean..." she began nervously. But Mary was not attending. Turning on her heel, she swept out to the vestibule.

Following her, Damaris saw her send a burning glance to her brother. Mary's chest was heaving, and she looked alarmingly pale—signs Damaris recognized. As a child, Mary had been much inclined toward tantrums if she did not get her own way. Obviously she was on the edge of one now. It was a pity that once they emerged into the street, the footman hurried to hand them into their carriage for, undoubtedly, Mary would not hesitate to give full rein to her fury and, in consequence, say a great many things she would later regret.

Damaris's fears proved all too accurate. Though Mary remained nervously silent while the coachman went through the intricate maneuvers attendant upon extricating the vehicle from the masses of carriages ranging all the way along King Street, once they had turned into St. James's Street, the storm broke.

In rising accents, Mary said, "I do not believe it would have been out of the way had I danced with Lord Bannerston. I have known him an age, and he was a dear friend of my husband's."

"If you will remember, Mary," Giles said calmly, "'twas your desire to *chaperone* Damaris. I did not believe it a good idea for you to come to the ball. I knew you'd not care to remain in the background with the dowagers."

"Prosy old hens!" Mary exploded.

"I remember saying as much to you," Giles continued, "and you assuring me that dancing could not be further from your mind."

"Emily Aldershot was attending balls not six months after they laid Aldershot in earth!" Mary snapped.

"An Aldershot is not a Harwine," Giles reminded her coldly.

Mary resorted to a favorite argument. "If Papa were alive, I doubt he'd be as top-lofty as you!"

"Since he is not, we may not ask him what he would do in a like circumstance."

"Actually, there would have been no need to consult him," Mary retorted. "I am not obliged to abide by your dictates, my dear brother. I am turned twenty-three, and I have long been of a mind to set up my own establishment!"

"Have you?" Giles inquired coldly. "Certainly I'll not stand in your way."

"You couldn't stand in my way. My plans are already set in motion." Mary darted a look at Damaris. "In fact, *we* have already selected a most desirable property in Park Place."

"Mary!" Damaris warned her.

"No, do not try to stop me." Mary glared at her. "I will speak. 'Tis time and past that he knew of it. Tomorrow, Giles, we will enter into negotiations with the agent."

"We? And to whom else might you be referring?" Giles demanded.

"I am referring to Damaris, who has agreed to live with me."

Damaris stiffened. She had been listening to their altercation with mixed emotions. Having a suspicion that Sir Francis's demise had left his widow only moderately grief-stricken, she understood Mary's resentment. Giles was arbitrary and proud. His regard for the Harwine name had been instilled in him at an early age, and with it, the sense of responsibility which had always set him apart from his siblings. Mary, on the other hand, was frivolous and fun-loving. Furthermore, having been wed to Sir Francis Gresham, she no longer needed to hold the Harwine banners aloft. Still, it had been foolish of her to blurt out her plans concerning that separate establishment now. Neither she nor Giles was in a reasonable mood. And what about herself? This afternoon she had been more than eager to escape from this house or, more specifically, from Giles. This evening she was of a different mind. . . .

"What may you mean by saying that Damaris cannot come with me? 'Tis all arranged," Mary said loudly.

Damaris jumped. Wrapped up in her own thoughts, she had not been attending to that heated exchange between brother and sister. They had all her attention now as Giles retorted, "Arrangements made without my sanction."

"And why must I have your sanction?" Mary demanded hotly. "Need I remind you that I am of age and—"

"Damaris is not. You seem to forget that she is my ward."

"I have not forgotten that," Mary returned, "but since she is past twenty and—"

"And will remain my responsibility until she is twenty-five."

"You cannot mean to abide by that ridiculous clause!"

"That is exactly what I mean to do." Giles glanced at Damaris. "I thought you aware of that, my dear."

"I *am* aware of it," Damaris said in a small voice. She was in a peculiar frame of mind—angry with Mary for disclosing plans which were hardly well-formulated, angry at Giles for adhering to a condition which she, too, found ridiculous.

"And will you force poor Damaris to remain here in single-blessedness until she's a spinster?" Mary demanded.

"It is up to me to see that she is protected—"

"Protected from *me!*" Mary cried furiously. "Damn you, I—"

"Mary," Giles said between gritted teeth, "the coach is drawing to a stop, which means we have arrived home. I would prefer it if you did not regale the footmen with your opinions of me."

Mary tossed her head defiantly. "You take too much upon yourself. You always have."

"I take no more than what is given me to take."

"If Papa were alive—"

"If he were alive, I cannot imagine he would countenance such a scheme. You are hardly the chaperone I would choose for Damaris, and..." He paused as the footman opened the door and pushed up the steps.

Mary was breathing hard. It was obvious that several heated retorts were crowding onto her tongue, but she managed to restrain them as Travers, looking weary and blinking against the candle he held in his thin, shaky hand, admitted them and lighted them to the second floor.

The butler's quavering goodnight moved Giles to say gently, "I have begged you to let Stanwell take over your duties late at night, Travers. Why will you not heed me?"

"Oh, no, my lord," the butler protested. "'Tis my duty, and I hope ye'll be all havin' a sound sleep."

"And the same to you, Travers." Giles had an affectionate look for him.

"Yes, Travers, good night," Damaris said.

"Good night, Travers." Mary watched impatiently as the old man slowly climbed the stairs to the third floor. Then, whirling on Giles, she said sharply, "You have no right—"

"On the contrary, I have every right," Giles interrupted, his cold gaze traveling from Mary to Damaris.

"'Tis a great pity that neither of you thought to consult me before entering into these negotiations. I might have saved you considerable time and trouble."

"But I . . . we . . ." Damaris began, pausing as she saw the chill expression in his eyes.

"You were about to say?" he prompted.

"Nothing."

"Very well, I shall bid you good evening." With the barest of nods, he went down the hall to his chamber.

Mary glared after him. "I beg you not to repine," she told Damaris. "I'll make all due arrangements with Mr. Grimsby upon the morrow, and we'll leave together!" Without giving Damaris a chance to respond, she retreated to her bedchamber.

Left alone in the hall, Damaris felt both anger and anguish. Her anger was all for Mary's ill-advised disclosures. Damaris had been primed to tell Mary exactly what she thought of such impulsive behavior, but even as the words had leaped to her lips, she had swallowed them. On occasion, she, too, had been similarly impulsive, and besides, Mary was in no mood to listen to reason.

What mattered was the look Giles had given her. Pondering it, Damaris guessed that he had felt betrayed. He probably believed that her new and inadvertently flirtatious manner had been initiated in hopes of persuading him to relax his supervision. He would never guess that, even given their differences, she could not help but like him, respect him, and . . .

Her fingernails bit into her palms. If there were only some way she could tell him that she had always been of two minds concerning Mary's plans to set up that separate establishment. It was too late for explanations. They would sound false. Her actions had been in line with the attitude of the Damaris he had known for most of his life.

She swallowed a lump in her throat. She sniffed and blinked. Touching her cheek, she found it wet and rubbed that revealing dampness away furiously. Tears would not help. They never did. Only one thing could have prevented this contretemps, and that would have been Giles's allowing Mary to waltz with Lord Bannerston!

CHAPTER
Four

DAMARIS LAY ON the chaise longue in her bedroom, studying a small pen-and-ink drawing of Vardon Hall, her former home in the north of England, near the Scottish border. She had taken the drawing from the mantel a few moments earlier. Ever since she could remember, it had stood there. She had glanced at it from time to time without its making any real impression on her, but last night her childhood home had figured in her dreams. She was not sure why. But, now that she had the drawing in hand, it gave rise to memories that had lain long dormant in her mind.

She had not seen Vardon Hall for seventeen years. Yet, she remembered there had been numerous trees in a large park that had also contained a lake. Her eyes returned to the picture of the house. She had a vague memory of dark paneled walls and of ragged banners attached to poles just beneath a vaulted ceiling. A hall? She did recall a huge stone fireplace large enough to roast an entire ox. And had there not been a long room, the walls of which were hung with portraits? Probably portraits in a gallery such as the one at Harwine Manor in Somerset.

Thinking about it now, it seemed amazing that she had never been back to her home. The house must have been standing empty for the last seventeen years! Of course, it would have a caretaker. Another memory flickered in her mind. Lord Harwine had spoken about taking her to Vardon Hall one summer, but something had intervened. Oh yes—Robert had climbed down from the bedroom window by hanging onto the jutting bricks and vines. He had fallen and broken his leg. The prank had kept him in bed for the rest of the summer and had much worried his parents. The following summer, Lord Harwine had become ill and—a tap on her door interrupted the flow of recollections.

"Yes?" she called.

"May I come in?" Mary asked.

Damaris tensed, wondering what Mary's mood must be. She herself did not want a recapitulation of last night's woes. Still, Mary's tempers were generally short-lived. "Yes, do come in."

Mary was dressed for the street in a green gown that spoke volumes for her mood. Furthermore, she was wearing green shoes and a green bonnet, and she was carrying a green reticule. The look in her green eyes was a blend of anger and defiance. She said, "Why have you kept to your room all this morning? I looked to see you much earlier."

"I did not waken until after one," Damaris explained. "I still feel tired." It was best not to mention that she had been feeling depressed and dispirited because of the quarrel with Giles, who, according to Travers, had left very early that morning.

"I don't feel tired—not in the least," Mary informed her coldly. "I have been out since nine. I have conferred with Mr. Grimsby, and I have also visited my man of business."

"Your man of buisness?"

"Yes, that is necessary since there are negotiations to be done. Fortunately, I do not have to depend on Mr. Mercer, whom the family employs. Francis had a very trustworthy man, and I am told that matters will go through easily. I should be able to move from here as soon as renovations are completed." She paused. "And will you come with me, my dear?"

"I am not sure that will be possible," Damaris replied, adding diffidently, "If you'd not spoken so prematurely..."

"Enough!" Mary ordered crossly. "No matter when I had broached the subject, I am sure Giles's answer would have been the same. It is all too obvious that he has the instincts of a tyrant and should like to keep the pair of us writhing under his thumb forever! You may writhe if you so choose, but I do not desire to be bound by his strictures." Mary shook a finger at Damaris. "You have only to pack your bandboxes and come with me. I do not think my dear brother would be of a mind to remove you forcibly. It would hardly add to his self-consequence, were the story to become known. Given the wagging tongues of the servants, it would probably be in the *Morning Post* by the time you'd hung up your coat. Come, Damaris, do say you'll leave this wretched prison!"

Damaris bit down a sigh. "I don't see how I may. Not at this time, Mary. You forget that Giles has charge of my fortune."

"He has no hold on mine!" Mary exclaimed. "And sure I have more than enough of the ready for the two of us." The glitter died out of her eyes. In a cajoling voice, she continued, "My dear, you cannot want me to be knocking about in that place all by myself. I should be so lonely."

A vivid image of being dependent upon Mary's generosity arose in Damaris's mind. From a child, Mary had never been generous. A succession of abigails had complained that she never parted with a gown unless it was so badly stained that it was unwearable or so moth-eaten that it was fit for naught save the scrap-bag: Furthermore, Mary's disposition was not of the best. Damaris had had ample proof of the fact that she had changed very little since the days when her moods had been the terror of the nursery. Even now, when she was obviously making an effort to be on her best behavior, her eyes were shooting forth sparks. All in all, there were enough straws in the wind for Damaris to be glad that Giles had taken the responsibility for refusing to move from off her shoulders. With an assumption of regret, she said, "I do think you should try and find some indigent cousin."

"Phoebe, perhaps?" Mary demanded sarcastically.

"There's also Lady Martha and that woman who was married to the Bishop of—"

"Dowds and bores!" Mary exclaimed angrily. "I take it you have no intention of abiding by your promise?"

"I don't see how it is possible."

"Well, Damaris, I must say that I never knew you were so monstrous poor-spirited." Turning on her heel, Mary stalked out. The fact that she did not slam the door indicated to Damaris only that she was in one of her venomous rather than furious moods.

Damaris returned to contemplation of the little picture. It occurred to her that now would be an ideal time to return to her old home. Such an action would provide a near solution to two of her most pressing problems. She would be relieved from the necessity of dealing with

Mary's angers and with Giles's marriage schemes. However, she remembered belatedly, she could go nowhere without Giles's consent. She released a short sigh and, rising, returned the picture to its place on the mantel.

She proceeded to the bookcase beside her bed and took our Mrs. Radcliffe's gothic novel, *The Italian* with the fixed ambition of forgetting her troubles by involving herself in those of its unfortunate heroine, Elena. However, despite such terrors as a sinister monk, blood-stained phantom hands, and mysterious strangers, Damaris found the tale heavy going. She retired to bed at the early hour of eight and fell asleep immediately.

Hours later, she was jolted from sleep by a sound out of a dream of Robert. No, not Robert, actually, but of the noise his pebbles used to make when hurled against her window. What had brought that to mind? She had not thought of Robert in a long time. Yet, inadvertently, she found her hand stealing up to her throat. She did not feel the golden chain on which she had hung his ring. She had removed it even before doffing her mourning. Ring and chain lay at the bottom of her jewel box. She had a tiny sigh for that. She had vowed never to remove it as long as she lived, but . . . She started, alerted by yet another sound, most unusual for so late an hour. Someone was hurling the knocker against its plate with considerable force over and over again.

Damaris sat up in bed, staring fearfully into the darkness. Who would be filling the house with that brazen clamor at such an hour? Perhaps she was dreaming that, too. Impossible! She slipped from bed and, flinging her peignoir over her shoulders, hurried to open her door. As she did, she heard old Travers grumbling to himself as he came slowly down the stairs from the third floor. She waited until he had clumped down the second flight of stairs and then hurried to the balustrade to peer into the darkness, relieved only by the flickering light from the butler's candle. As she stood waiting, she heard Travers open the small peephole in the door, heard him cry out, and suddenly the bolt was drawn.

"What's amiss? What are you doing from your bed?"

Startled, Damaris turned to see Giles wearing his brocade dressing gown hurrying toward her. He carried a candle, and its flame, reflected in his eyes, brought back a fugitive memory of another night when . . . Damaris stiffened as she heard louder cry from the butler, followed by a sobbing rush of words, "I could 'ardly believe it were ye . . . Oh, Master Robbie, oh, my dear, dear lad, ye've come 'ome at last."

Someone else had cried out. The sound was in her ears. Who had it been? Her throat was smarting. Suddenly Giles had set his candle down on a nearby table. His arm was around her waist, supporting her, holding her against him. His voice was in her ear.

"Do not swoon, my dear," he was saying very gently, as if he were no longer angry with her, while from two flights down, a voice drifted up to them, a voice filled with emotion. "Well, Travers, well, well, well," someone was saying.

Damaris tore herself from Giles's restraining grasp and ran to the stairs. Not heeding his warning cry and unmindful of the darkness, she dashed down to the ground floor. The hall was thick with shadows cast by the wavering light in the butler's candle, but it was not so dark that she could not see the tall man in the many-caped coat, could not exclaim breathlessly, "Robert, oh, it is you!"

Moments later, the four of them—Giles, Damaris, Mary, and Robert—were seated in the library. A decanter of brandy stood on the table. Each of them clutched a glass of the golden liquid. They had just toasted Robert, and Damaris was uncomfortably sure that all three of them shared the same emotion—a pity which she devoutly hoped was not reflected on their faces.

Mary was very near tears. Giles's features were in shadow, and Damaris felt as if her own were rigid as she looked at Robert's scarred countenance and at the black patch that covered his left eye. He'd been blinded in that eye by the bayonet slash that had cut him from hairline to jaw. The scar was a dusky red. It had puckered his cheek, and in healing pulled his mouth slightly out of alignment.

Oddly enough, the wound was not totally disfiguring. It had merely imparted a rakish, devil-may-care look that was actually appealing. In fact, Damaris thought, he resembled the drawing of a pirate used to illustrate one of Byron's poems. Yet, how dreadfully he must have suffered! Her heart went out to him even though she was sure he would never court her pity. In fact, he seemed just like his old self—gay, heedless, and charming. There had been only two really emotional moments—when he had learned why his father and mother were not there to greet him; and when he had kissed them all, saying afterwards, much in the manner of old Travers, "Well, I am home at last."

Subsequently, he had asked for the brandy they were drinking, had a glass with the butler, and sent him up to bed. He was now preparing to answer what he had teasingly described as "Brother Giles's inevitable questions as to why you've not heard from me for two years?"

Tilting back in his chair, Robert continued, "For a long time, the only thing I remembered was waking up in a wagon filled with corpses to be dumped in a pit for burial."

"Oh, no!" Mary murmured.

"Come, come, love." Robert bent a censorious eye upon her. "This is war. If you're going to be squeamish, you'd best have the tale secondhand tomorrow."

Mary made a face at him and stuck out her tongue, which made them all laugh. It also served to lessen the tension, Damaris thought gratefully.

"Anyhow," Robert continued, "an orderly, bless him, noticed that, though somewhat the worse for wear, I was still very much alive. And so I was hauled along to a tent where an American doctor was sawing off limbs with great abandon. Much to my surprise, he did not attack my arm—even though there was a ball through it. He extracted the bullet, but he couldn't do a thing for my eye or for my memory."

"Your memory?" Giles demanded.

"Yes, it had flown where . . . where memories go. Once I was patched up a bit, I was put in a prison that lay just over the border from Canada. Ghastly place. The worst part of it was that I was incarcerated with some troops who hadn't the least notion where my own company was so they couldn't identify me."

"What was the prison like?" Mary asked.

"Suffice to say that I hope you never find out," he answered with a twisted smile. "At any rate, a few brave lads and I escaped, and what with crawling through sloughs of despond and lakes of fire I became ill again and was nursed back to health by some farm people. I stayed with them, helping out with the chores, until one day I fell and hit my head on a rock. After that I began to have dreams." His eye lingered on Damaris's face. "I dreamed of you, my dear. And one day I found myself saying 'Dam' and 'twas not swearing—for the rest of your name followed, and with it my memory."

"Oh," she breathed, meeting his glance. She did not know how she felt, save that it was wonderful to see him again and to know that he was alive.

"Once my memory was back, I bade good-bye to my farmers and was loaded with cheeses and a ham. They were good people. Two weeks later, I reached Fort Niagara, only to be told that my regiment had marched to New York.

"I wanted to join them, but I was much weakened by

my journey, which had been undertaken on foot, I being without resources save for the few pennies my benefactors were able to give me. My shoulder was stiff and I was still suffering from headaches. The commander of the fort and the company surgeon urged me to sell out. I was reluctant to take this advice, but they insisted, and so I did. I came home on the first available ship, which was the *Prometheus*. We docked at Portsmouth, and— here I am."

"Why didn't you write?" Giles demanded.

"I did write," Robert responded. "I wrote as soon as I could lay my hand on quill and paper." He frowned. "That orderly looked half-starved. 'Tis possible he ate the missive." His laugh was not successful. He added somberly, "At least I am here. There was a time . . . but no need to talk of that."

"Oh, God!" Mary said brokenly. "If only we'd known you were alive. We were in agony."

"I, too, was in agony, my dearest, knowing that you must have been informed of my death. I knew Mama would be beside herself and Father . . ." He paused and swallowed. "I think I am glad I knew no more."

Silence fell upon the little group, and Damaris, looking at Robert, met his eye and found it abrim with unshed tears. She longed to rush to his side and comfort him, but of course she could not do that—not with Giles sitting at the desk.

Giles.

He had moved and she could see his face. Suddenly she remembered his arms around her waist and his voice urging her not to swoon. He had been so kind, so caring. Yet, at the same time, there had been a distance, as if in touching her he had at the same time drawn back spiritually. Did he believe that she was still in love with Robert?

How could he believe anything else? Hadn't she told

him that her heart was buried with Robert? He hadn't believed it then, but did he believe it now?

Her heart did not need to lie in a grave, not when that grave was unoccupied. Amazingly, incredibly, Robert was alive! Yet, it was very difficult to believe that she was not dreaming.

Damaris pressed her hands against the carvings of her chair; her palms hurt. She was not dreaming, had not been dreaming when she had heard the pebbles strike the glass.

Robert had been throwing pebbles at her window as he had always done. Did that mean that his feelings were unchanged? Of course it meant that. Had he not explained that a vision of her had helped restore his memory? He had really been saying that he loved her as much as ever.

She looked up and found him gazing at her with that one eye—poor eye—and then she caught sight of Giles. His expression was enigmatic. What was he thinking? That he would not need to seek very far afield for her bridegroom?

How very convenient for Giles, she thought bitterly. Soon, very soon, he would be relieved of the responsibilities he had inherited from his father. He could concentrate on seeking a bride. She thought of Almack's and all those languishing ladies. He could have his pick, but which one would he choose? She did not want to dwell on that—better to think of her own situation. Would it be resolved soon? Did she really want such resolutions? She had no answers—but surely some manner of enlightenment must come.

During the two days following Robert's return from what Mary insisted on calling "the dead," the enlightenment Damaris sought remained elusive. And, somewhat to her surprise, so did Robert. On his first morning home, he went off to see the commander of his old regiment. Subsequently, he went to visit some of his cronies in that same regiment. He returned in time to partake of a festive meal served by Mrs. Kimball, the cook, who had exerted herself especially on behalf of Mr. Robbie, whom, she tearfully told anyone who would listen, she had known since a lad when he used to steal cakes from the kitchen windowsill.

On his second day home, he had visited the family physician in the morning. His afternoon had been spent in the library with Giles, a conference from which he emerged in no very good humor. That night he had made one of a party of four of his old friends and had sallied forth for a night on the town.

This morning Robert and Giles had gone out together and returned with the information that they had purchased a fine saddle horse for Robert at Tattersall's. Consequently, the conversation at the midday meal had been very horsy, with Robert drawing amusing comparisons between American steeds and the better British mounts. Giles had left the table early and gone to the library to look over some papers prior to a meeting with his man of business, and Mary had proposed that she, Robert, and Damaris go for a walk in Hyde Park.

Damaris, who had been hoping that she and Robert might have spent the afternoon talking, had half-expected him to refuse. But he had acquiesced eagerly, and she had begun to think herself wrong about his soft glances upon his arrival. She had even wondered if he might not have found a girl in Canada to whom he had given his heart. She could not imagine Robert living for two years without some manner of female companionship.

Now, as the three of them walked along the street, Damaris was once more confused. They were not going in the direction of the Park because Mary wanted him to see her house. As they came within sight of it, she said defensively, "In a sense, we are at the Park since this building is in Park Place."

"Very neat, my love." Robert silently clapped his hands and Mary made one of her faces at him. "Ah," he winked at her, "'Tis quite like old times, pulling the wool over Giles's eyes."

His remark confused Damaris. "Why is it necessary to do that?"

Robert's eye was bright with amusement. "Why is it not?" His laughter fled suddenly. "I hope you've not put yourself on the side of the angels."

"Poor child, she's had no choice," Mary said. "I've told you how it is."

"Your guardian!" Robert shook his head. "Lord, my father must have been in his dotage."

"He was nothing of the kind," Damaris cried hotly.

"No," Mary said soberly, "that's not true, Robbie."

He had turned equally sober. "I am sure not. I should not have said it. Giles was his only choice and 'twas a good one. My brother is trustworthy, if tiresome."

Damaris opened her mouth to argue and closed it as Mary brought the key to the front door out of her reticule. A few moments later, they had come through the small hall into the drawing room.

"Good Lord!" Robert exclaimed looking around. "Have matters worsened so much between you and Giles that you must come *here?*"

"Do not turn your nose up quite so high. You'll find this room will be entirely different when that ghastly paper's removed and I've substituted green and white stripes and the most beautiful Chippendale mirror and—"

"Please, dear Mary." He held up a protesting hand. "I know your taste is unexceptional, but what has occurred to put our worthy brother's back up?"

"I have told you." Mary sighed. "Do you never listen?"

"Perhaps I am still having trouble with my memory."

"Very well, here's a hint. Almack's."

"Ah, Bannerston."

Mary flushed. "Not Lord Bannerston in particular...dancing," she emphasized. "You know Francis wouldn't have wanted me to sit in a corner."

"He'd have been wiser than to expect so great a sacrifice, my love. Poor Francis was a downy bird."

"You are horrid," Mary scolded. "But"—she smiled—"'tis lovely having you here again."

"'Tis twice as lovely to be back, my angel." His glance wandered over to Damaris, who had retreated to her favorite windowsill. "Thrice as lovely," he murmured.

Mary laughed. "Well, my dears," she said, "I'm off to the bootmaker."

"The...bootmaker?" Damaris echoed.

"Yes." Mary was avoiding her glance. "I have ordered several pairs of half-boots in the most exquisite leathers." She turned to Robert. "I pray you'll excuse me, brother dearest."

"Your prayers are granted, most divine of sisters." He bowed. "And though you've not asked it of me, I shall see Damaris home."

"I had hoped that would be understood." Mary smiled at Damaris. "Au revoir."

"But Mary, you said nothing," Damaris began, pausing as Mary hurried into the hall. A second later she heard the door slam behind her. Turning back, Damaris found Robert smiling. A suspicion crossed her mind. "You did not come to see this house," she accused him.

"No," he agreed. "I came so that I might be private with you, my sweetest angel. And I hope you'll join me in blessing Mary for her kindness."

"We could have been private at home," Damaris said hesitantly. "Giles is in the city."

"He could return...when he's least expected." Robert's smile vanished. "When I recovered my memory, I found I remembered a great deal—including what might have been our last night together. Do you remember that, my love?"

"Yes." Damaris looked down at her hands.

"Here we'll have no interruptions from importunate brothers. Here we'll remain undisturbed, which is all to the good—for I have much I wish to say." He strolled toward her but at the last moment he changed course and sat down on the opposite windowsill. Looking at her intently, he continued, "I expect you find me much changed." He ran a finger over the patch that hid his eye, then traced the scar from cheek to jaw. "Handsome Robbie's gone away."

Damaris noted a bitter twist to his lip and heard a deeper bitterness in his voice. A knot of pity formed in her breast. "I do not see that he's away," she said gently, "I see only that he's come back."

He leaned forward and seized her hand, carrying it to his lips. "Oh, God," he said, still holding it, "thank you for that, my dearest. I've been thinking you'd find me a poor thing compared with what I once was."

"How could you think that would make any difference to me?" Damaris said indignantly. "Surely you know me better than that."

"Ah," he breathed. "Then you haven't changed."

That question gave her pause. It could mean so much and yet how might she answer save with the negation that was, in itself an affirmation. It was impossible for her to resist the appeal in his one remaining eye. "No," she said.

A long breath escaped him. "And I feared you'd be wed," he said.

"Oh, no!" she breathed.

"Is there a reason why you're not wed, Damaris?" he demanded softly.

She had the impression he knew the answer to his

question, that his helpful sister Mary had primed him as to the reasons behind her prolonged mourning—and must have described the mourning as well... "Yes."

"It cannot be for want of admirers. You are even more beautiful than I'd remembered, and that is odd, for your face has haunted my dreams. As you know, it brought me back to reality." He groaned. "God, if you knew how frightened I was when I awakened from that long spell of emptiness to find myself so much changed and you an ocean distant. Then—" he smiled at her lovingly— "to come home and find you are still Miss Vardon. Why?" He rose and stood looking down at her. "Tell me, why you are still Miss Vardon, Damaris."

He wanted to hear what he knew to be the truth. It *ought* to have been the truth. If only he had returned a month earlier... but her feeling for him could not have altered in so brief a span, not when she had agonized over his passing for so long.

Yet she had an odd feeling that there was a chasm between the Damaris of this moment and the girl who had gone about in deepest mourning, making an effort to weep into her pillow every night. It was not a chasm of space, but of time. She felt immeasurably older than the Damaris of two months ago. That self had childishly prolonged emotions and attitudes that she ought to have abandoned months, even a year, before. She had been playing a part. It had been fun to pretend.

Had she really been so foolish? Had she really known that she had outgrown her love for Robert? She could not be sure. She could only be sure that it was gone and that another had supplanted it—another which, in a sense, was almost as arid as loving the dead.

Giles did not want her. He only wanted her to make an advantageous marriage. Well, she would marry Robert, and that ought to please him. Robert had asked her a question. She must answer with that old truth she had once believed, but in all honesty she could not tell him she still loved him. Still, she need not tell him anything about the state of her heart. She said in a low voice, "I am sure you know why I am still unwed, Robert."

"Oh, God, Damaris!" he said in a choked whisper. He caught her to him, and she was frightened momentarily, remembering the roughness with which he had treated her that last night. However, his kiss was gentle, very gentle.

She put her arms around him. She *did* feel something for him. She felt sorry for all that he had suffered. She wanted to comfort him, cherish him, keep him from all harm. But a wiser Damaris whispered in her ear that those emotions were the sentiments of a mother, not a sweetheart, not a wife. She would need to be careful that he never discovered her secret.

CHAPTER
Five

"I THINK NOT, Robert," Giles said decisively. He was seated behind the desk in the library.

Watching him, Damaris wished she were a thousand miles away. Because of Robert's insistence that she be present when he offered for her hand, she was sitting in her accustomed chair, her hands on the lion heads, thinking that their snarling features were not much different from those of the man she had decided she must love.

"You think not, Giles. Why not?" Robert demanded.

"I am sure you recall our father's reasons for refusing to sanction the match. The situation has not changed. Damaris is still an heiress, while you have, as yet, little in the way of prospects. I know you are not a fortune hunter but—"

"Damn you!" Robert leaped to his feet. "You know I love her...have been cruelly separated from her for two years, and you dare to hint that...that her fortune means anything to me?"

"He has just said that he knows it does not, Robert," Damaris reminded him.

He emitted a short bark of a laugh. "You are naïve if you believe he means what he has just said. He is suggesting that I want only your money and naught else—when, in fact, I had forgotten that you were an heiress." He glared at Giles. "I know you will not credit that. What can you know of love?"

A protest leaped to Damaris's lips at a question she could only consider heartless—unless Robert, in his anger, had forgotten Lady Laura. She wanted to apologize to Giles, but, on looking at him, she found herself facing a stare so chill that she shivered, inadvertently.

Giles said in a low voice, "I have known what it is to love. I have also known the pain that comes with its loss and—"

"I am sorry," Robert interrupted brusquely. "I did not mean—"

"Never mind that now." Giles was equally brusque. "I want you to know that I am not giving you an unequivocal refusal. I am taking into account the fact that you do seem to have remained constant, and I do recall Father saying that, if you were still of the same mind when you returned from the wars, he would not stand in your way. Nor shall I. But I happen to believe that he would agree you must be situated in a way that would not force you to depend on your bride's inheritance."

"But you have said that he left me twenty thousand pounds. That does not make me a pauper."

"True, but it is not enough to last a lifetime. Indeed, such sums have been lost at Watier's and White's in a single night—in a single hour of play. And since you have always had extravagant tastes—"

"All that is changed," Robert interrupted.

"Perhaps. But before I sanction this marriage, I would like more evidence of that change."

"And how will you obtain that—save through years of watching?" Robert's lip curled. "You say that I may marry Damaris. When? How long will this...observation of yours endure?"

"No more than a year."

"A year!" Robert groaned. "A year when we are longing—"

"I beg you to listen to me," Giles interrupted patiently. "You have resigned your commission and I am glad of that. I have never approved of a lifetime spent on one battlefield or another. However, since I am not able to give you more than the money left to you in Father's will, it would seem to me that you must enter another field of endeavor."

"You're suggesting that I become a curate or—"

"No, I cannot believe you cut out for that life." A small smile played about Giles's mouth and vanished as he continued. "There are other avenues open to you. As you know, we have considerable holdings in Dorset— farms, mainly. I am in need of a reliable man who can maintain the property and—"

"An estate agent, in fact?" Robert regarded him incredulously. "You'd offer *me* such a position?"

"It is not uncommon for a younger son to serve in such a capacity," Giles said earnestly.

"Serve." Robert's jaw was working, and his face was distorted with fury. "I am not minded toward being your servant, Giles."

"Robert," Damaris said warningly, "you are being unreasonable."

"And is *he* not being unreasonable?" Robert demanded hotly. "Is he not discounting the fact that I love you, that

I can scarce bear to be in your company without wanting you? And...and he speaks of some damned apprenticeship in *Dorset*. Overseeing the milking of cows, perchance?"

"I did not mention an apprenticeship," Giles retorted. "I said I would put you in *charge* of the properties. The farms and the livestock are in the hands of the tenantry. And if, in a year, you proved capable, I would not only give you my permission to wed Damaris, I would also give you the estate as well."

"A year, *twelve* months." Robert groaned. "It could as well be twelve centuries. Can you not realize what Damaris means to me?"

Damaris kept her eyes on her lap, on her clenched hands. She had not expected Giles to object so strenuously to the hasty wedding Robert had proposed. She had thought he must be glad to be rid of her.

For her part, she had reconciled herself to the thought of wedding Robert. After all, he loved her passionately— something Giles probably could not understand. Or had he loved Lady Laura passionately? She doubted it. Passion seemed foreign to his nature. That was why she dared not imagine that he had any ulterior motive in forbidding the banns. However, it would be well if she and Robert could be married sooner. Then, she would not need to remain in the same house with Giles, seeing him every day and wanting...She gritted her teeth. She must not dwell on impossibilities. She fixed her eyes on Robert, who *did* want her.

He was glaring at Giles, who was saying, "I should think you'd love Damaris too much to want to be dependent on such monies as she would bring to you."

"Good God!" Robert's face was flushed and his scar glowed an even deeper red, emphasizing his fury. "I...you..." He paused and swallowed. "Were you not my brother..." Raising clenched fists, he brought them down on the desk with a force that caused a book to tumble to the floor and some of the fluid to splash from an open inkwell. Robert moved back hastily as Giles took out his handkerchief and mopped up the spill hurriedly. Robert stared down at it and then added furiously, "That's what you have in your damned veins—ink!" Turning on his heel, he stalked out of the room, slamming the door behind him.

Damaris rose. Looking at Giles, she said tentatively, "I am sorry. Your offer was entirely within the bounds of reason. I am sure that when Robert comes to his senses . . ."

Giles held up an inkstained hand. "My dear, I think you must offer that consolation where 'tis wanted most. I am of the opinion that your distraught lover is more in need of comforting than I. I give you leave to attend him. Meanwhile, I must see that this fine piece of furniture loses none of its polish."

Damaris stiffened, hearing mockery in his tone and seeing amusement in his eyes. All her old animosity toward him arose anew. "You find something to laugh about in this situation? I think I must agree with Robert. You *do* have ink in your veins!" Whirling, she ran out of the room, not neglecting to slam the door with even more force than that employed by his brother. Before she could take another step, she had been caught in Robert's embrace.

"My love, my dearest," he murmured, his lips against her hair, "there'll be a way out of this farrago. We'll be wed, and soon. You may be assured of that for I am convinced I cannot live without you."

They were at supper, Giles, Robert, Mary, and Damaris—the children, as Mrs. Kimball had put it to Travers. Damaris had heard the cook, her eyes full of sentimental tears, saying, "An' 'tis good to see them all together, though 'tis a shame Lady Deborah could not be with them, so far away in Scotland."

Damaris had good reason to remember that remark, good reason to think about Scotland, also, but she was considering many things, including the quarrel in the library of the previous week. While a certain coldness remained in Giles's manner toward her, it was no more chill than her own attitude toward him. He and Robert were on better terms, due mainly to Robert's promise to visit the properties in Dorset within the month. Mary was also in Giles's good graces for agreeing that he was right in recommending such a good course. Her elder brother had pronounced himself highly gratified by this unexpected support.

Damaris gazed at Giles from under lowered lashes. As usual, he sat at the head of the table. There was a serenity to his countenance that brought his father to mind. With a little shock, Damaris recalled that he was the head of the family. He was young to hold that position. Too young, she thought bitterly, to be understanding. She was in reluctant agreement with Robert. The late Lord Harwine would never have kept them apart—not after Robert's terrible ordeal in Canada. Furthermore, he would have looked upon his younger son with an eye unclouded by the rivalry that had always existed between the brothers.

She was sure Giles had much resented the fact that Robert was his mother's favorite. Yet, how small of him to let that old resentment prejudice him at this late date—unless it was more than that. But she had promised not to dwell on such possibilities. In suggesting that their marriage plans be postponed, Giles was only being cautious—and that caution was misplaced. Robert *had* changed. He was much calmer, much more responsible. She was sure he would have managed the Dorset holdings very well. But now he must oversee her estate.

She shivered. Northumberland was so very far away. It would take between two and three days to reach the Hall, longer if it rained—as it might. The weather was known to be extremely inclement in the Border country. However, they were not going *directly* to the Hall, she reminded herself. Their initial destination must be Gretna Green. Damaris looked down, not wanting Giles to see her face for fear he might read the mixture of excitement and trepidation which might be mirrored in it and wonder at her mood, since this was to be an evening passed at home.

Making conversation had been very difficult during this meal. She knew it had been just as difficult for Mary, who was much flushed and had been given to giggling over nothing. Robert, soon to be her own husband, seemed amazingly calm. Prevarication had always come easily to him, and tonight he was inspired. He had been talking about various breeds of cattle as if he intended to visit the nearest fair and purchase stock. Giles was listening closely and occasionally giving him the benefit of what he had learned over the years.

Damaris was certain he did not suspect, that anything out of the ordinary would be underway that night. They had been planning the elopement for the last six days, and every detail had been worked out most meticulously. The plan would be put into operation directly after Giles left for Watier's, whence he was accustomed to go every Thursday night to play piquet with an old friend.

"'Tis well my brother's such a creature of habit," Robert had said with a trace of contempt.

Damaris had resented that remark, resented the contempt. Giles might be staid and serious, but he was also dependable. She shot another look at him. He was still deep in conversation with Robert, smiling and animated as he talked knowledgeably about the merits of Hereford cows as opposed to Ayrshires or Devons.

Damaris felt a constriction in her chest, realizing that this was the last time she would ever see him so situated at the head of the table in the bosom of that family, which would be gone by the time he returned from his card game. Giles would never, never forgive them for this breach of trust! She would have difficulty forgiving herself—but she *must* put such thoughts from her mind. She had determined upon her course and must abide by that decision. Still, she did not like to contemplate his reactions when he found them missing. Possibly he would not discover their absence until the following morning and then . . . what? Would he guess that they had fled to Gretna Green? Despite her urging, Robert would not let her leave a note for Giles.

"Depend upon it, my love, if he received such a missive, he would immediately guess we were on our way to Scotland. He would be after us posthaste, trailing us all the way across the Border."

Damaris winced. Somehow the idea of leaving Giles ignorant of their purpose seemed cruel and ungrateful, but what other choice did they have? Were he to follow them, he might challenge Robert to a duel—no, probably it would be the other way around—but still it would be terrible, brother fighting brother over herself. And if any harm should come to Giles . . . She shuddered. Robert was right. It was far better that he should be deceived.

And when Giles finally knew the truth, what would he do?

Of course, he would not know that for some time, because she was sure he would never guess they had gone to her estate. He had probably forgotten its existence. No, she was certain he had not. As her guardian, it fell under his jurisdiction, and he was a responsible man. Most likely, he required the bailiff to send him monthly reports. She wished she might have seen those. Perhaps they would have helped refresh her memory of the place. Would it be like Harwine Keep in Somerset? No, the drawing suggested that it was of an entirely different shape. She sighed. She loved Harwine Keep, but now would never see it again, never ride in its vast park, never travel to Glastonbury, which was but a few miles distant, to wander around the abbey ruins and dream of King Arthur and his knights. It would be difficult not to see it again, but her own home had its own beauties. In the drawing the park looked small, but she was sure it was extensive. She had vague memories of it.

"A penny for your thoughts, Damaris."

She started and stared at Giles. "What . . . ?"

"You are looking very pensive," he commented. "Would a half-crown be more to your liking?"

She felt her face burning, knew it must be fiery red, and said crossly, "I wasn't really thinking about anything." She forced a little titter of a laugh. "Consequently, my thoughts are worth nothing."

His green gaze lingered on her face. "I would never say that, my dear. You've been very quiet tonight, and, as they say, still waters run deep."

Mary giggled. "La, what should she be thinking, pray?"

Giles's eyes rested on Damaris. "Evidently she is not of a mind to tell me."

Damaris had turned cold. Did Giles suspect that something was afoot? Had Mary's constant giggling alerted him? But Mary always giggled. He could not suspect anything. He had just been teasing her, as usual, damn him. She would not be sorry to see him depart. She wished . . . she wished they were out of the house and on the Great North Road to Scotland.

"I thought," Mary remarked with a roll of her eyes, "that dinner would never end. Giles was in an unusually expansive mood, but of course he would be, thinking he'd won a victory. It was droll to hear Robbie waxing so knowledgeable over cows. I was hard put not to burst out laughing."

"You did laugh quite a bit," Damaris reminded her.

"I do not imagine Giles thought it out of the way, since I'd told him how much I approved his plans for Robbie. Lord, how could he think Robbie would abide by his ridiculous demands? He must think him as poor-spirited as himself."

Damaris, who had been fastening her cloak, dropped her hands and faced Mary. "I do not believe Giles poor-spirited. Do you recall that day in the Park, the nau-machia, when he did not hesitate to strike a man twice his size?"

"Perhaps mean-spirited would be the better description," Mary conceded with a shrug. "I am delighted to be leaving this house, I can tell you, and 'twill be rare sport to have you and Robbie with me at Park Place. You must agree."

Damaris forced a smile. But what Mary insisted on terming the "fatal hour" approached, she was far more frightened than excited. She was glad she had elected to stay in Mary's room because she had spirit enough for them both. In fact, Mary was far more titillated at the prospect of the elopement than Damaris, and no wonder! It had been her suggestion, offered on the evening of the day Giles had issued his ultimatum.

At that moment, Damaris had been so angry with him that she would have left within the hour, which would have served him right for his horrid attitude. However, during the ensuing days, second thoughts had kept oc-curring, and as of this morning, there had been third and fourth thoughts crowding into her mind. She was hard put to rid herself of them.

Once she and Robert were on the road, she hoped she would begin to be excited. There *was* something partic-ularly thrilling at the thought of a coach-and-four speeding out of London at the hour of midnight. It would not be precisely midnight—but it would be ten, and the moon high in the sky. She glanced at the clock, and her heart gave a frenzied leap. It wanted but ten minutes of the hour. Where was Betsy, Mary's abigail, a silly, lackadasical creature, much given to dawdling. She ought to be returning from her post as lookout for the coach Robert had gone to fetch. Indeed, she should be here by now.

"Mary," Damaris said tensely, "'tis time."

Mary, who had been adjusting her bonnet before her mirror, gave Damaris a consoling glance over her shoulder. "I should not worry," she said easily. "We could not expect Robbie to be here precisely at the stroke of ten."

"I hope there's been nothing untoward to delay him," Damaris said.

"Untoward? What could you mean?" Mary asked.

"The streets are rife with footpads."

"Bless you, child, he's not coming here alone. There'll be a coachman with a musket beneath his seat and postillions with pistols in their pockets."

"Perhaps," Damaris murmured, "'twould be better if we waited below."

"We cannot chance that," Mary said decisively. "As I told you before, if one or another of the servants were about . . . Drat that Betsy, where can she be?" Annoyance suddenly filled Mary's tone.

"Oh, dear, I wish we might have entrusted Sara with that errand." Damaris thought of her abigail with some distress. She had made a show of going to bed very early and had dismissed the girl quickly. Sara had seemed surprised. Had she been suspicious? Sara would be much distressed and hurt when she found Damaris had gone without her, but Mary had insisted that Betsy must suffice for both of them. "There will be three of us in the coach, and if it rains Robert will not want to ride outside and 'twill be crowded." She had not added that Betsy was most skillful at arranging Mary's bronze locks, Damaris thought resentfully.

"Of course," Mary began and paused as the clock began to chime the hour.

"Hssst," Damaris whispered. "I hear footsteps on the stairs."

"I did not ... yes, there." Mary nodded.

Both women tensed, listening.

"They are too heavy to be those of Betsy," Mary whispered.

"Would Robert have come to fetch us?"

"'Twas not the plan."

"A servant?" Damaris hazarded.

"Possibly. Damn the man, I hope he's bound for the third floor."

Damaris held her breath, waiting, hoping that the footsteps would continue across the hall. Then a strange sound reached her ears. *A click.* "What's that?" she whispered. "Oh, God!" she added and knew exactly what it had been. She rushed to the door, twisted the knob, and pulled.

"What are you doing?" Mary demanded.

"I cannot open the door!" Damaris turned wide, terrified eyes on Mary. "It's l-locked!"

"Locked?" Mary repeated blankly. "But 'tis impossible. There's no one here would dare do such a thing!"

"I heard the lock catch," Damaris said dully.

"I didn't. It must be jammed. Let me open it, love." Mary turned the knob and then began to shake and pull at it. "You're right."

"But who ... what ... oh, Lord, Giles must have guessed. But how could he?" Damaris cried. "And what will Robert think? What will he do?"

Mary administered a furious kick to the door and groaned at the damage done to her toe. "We must get out!" she cried, pounding the door with both fists. Damaris, joining her, also pounded. They called Giles's name. They screamed it. Mary, who had had the benefit of a soldier's company, unleashed a string of colorful curses in Spanish, French, and English invoking several forms of eternal damnation upon her brother's head—all to no avail. The offending portal remained locked all night.

Several hours after dawn, Damaris, curled up in a chair, awakened once again to find that she was still locked into Mary's chamber. But this time she heard something. Blearily, she looked around the room and discovered that the door was opening. A slight snore turned her attention toward the bed where Mary, still in her cloak, lay in an exhausted slumber. Damaris shuddered. The day of reckoning was upon them—or should she call it the "day of wrath"?

"Oh—Miss Damaris."

Damaris turned toward the door and saw her abigail standing just beyond the threshold, looking at her nervously. "Yes, Sara?"

"Please, miss, his lordship would like it if you and . . . her ladyship would—would attend him in the library within fifteen minutes, please."

"You may tell his lordship," Damaris began grandly and then paused. Considering the circumstances, there was nothing Sara could tell his lordship, save that they would be there. She continued shortly. "That we will join him as soon as we have . . . made ourselves presentable. Once you've given him that information, please come back to my chamber immediately, Sara."

"Oh yes, miss." Sara hurried away.

Damaris drew a long breath and went to wake up Mary.

Twenty minutes later, Mary and Damaris were seated in a pair of chairs facing Giles, who was ensconced behind his desk, regarding them with what Damaris could only describe as contempt. "You must think," he was saying, "that I am extraordinarily thick-headed. Else you surely could not have imagined that I should be taken in by Robert's patently spurious interest in livestock. Even had he been as consummate an actor as the great David Garrick, he had scant help from his—er—supporting cast. You, Mary, were giggling like a ninny, and you, Damaris, looked so apprehensive that one might have believed you in fear of the immediate entrance of the devil—without costume and makeup. Consequently, my suspicions were alerted and I told my coachman to drive off while I lingered in the garden. And what was my reward? I saw my brother, clad in a traveling cloak, hurrying forth upon some—mysterious mission, followed a short time later by Mary's abigail, who, at my prompting, disclosed the scheme."

"So you locked us in," Mary said bitterly.

"And so I did, Mary," Giles acknowledged.

"And what of—Robbie?" Mary demanded.

"I believe he is staying at the King's Rest near Chelsea."

"You—you turned him out of the house?" she cried.

Giles nodded. "It seemed the best way to handle the situation." He glanced at Damaris, who shivered at the sight of his cold, accusing stare. "I am loath to cause you grief, my dear, but as your guardian, I cannot in conscience' sake countenance such an alliance."

Mary looked on the verge of hysteria. "But what was poor Robbie to do, with you bent on cruelly separating them and for a whole year!"

Giles's gaze grew even colder. "I take exception to your employment of the term 'cruel,' Mary. I am sure that neither my father nor Damaris's late parent would have wanted her to wed a man so lacking in moral character as to propose a clandestine marriage."

With rare bravery, Mary said, "'Twas I who proposed it—'twas my idea!"

"I do not doubt that. It is precisely the kind of scheme that would appeal to a woman as addicted to romantic trash from the Minerva Press as yourself. But Robert need not have accepted your suggestions. That he did so shows him sadly wanting in scruples."

"But...but you cannot cast him off! He is your brother!"

"And you are my sister," Giles returned coldly, his implications all too plain.

Mary drew herself up. "I wish I were not and, since I am obviously *de trop,* I shall leave this house as soon as my bandboxes are packed. Furthermore, I sincerely hope that I might have the great good fortune never to look upon your face again."

"I would hesitate to interfere with any decision you would make, Mary," Giles replied.

"Oh, Mary, no," Damaris cried. "Oh, Giles, you cannot mean to...to cast her off like that."

"It is her decision," he repeated stonily.

"I shall be gone within the hour," Mary snapped.

"Very well." Giles nodded. "Only I must ask you not to give vent to your temper and slam the door as you leave this room. Such an action would reflect only on your pronounced lack of discipline."

Mary glared at him furiously and did not respond to this dangerously provocative request—but the resulting crash of a door held back as far as it would go and then pushed forward with all the strength she could summon provided answer enough.

Damaris had put her hands to her ears. But Giles, seemingly undisturbed by the act he had instigated, turned his eyes on her. She winced as she saw that they were filled with both disappointment and accusation. "Since you seem bent on traveling," he said, "I have made arrangements to fulfill your wishes."

Damris flushed. "I...I want you to know that..." She paused and, meeting his contemptuous stare, the words froze on her lips. Obviously, he was in no mood to believe anything she had to tell him. "I am not really of a mind to travel," she said. Would that give him a hint of her real feelings?

"I am sorry for that, my dear," Giles replied, "but I think I must adhere to my particular schedule. I shall escort you, your abigail, and Cousin Phoebe—"

"Cousin Phoebe!" Damaris looked at him in horror.

"Yes," he returned blandly. "Early this morning I dispatched a footman to her house asking her if she'd be willing to assume the position of chaperone once again— beginning immediately. She sent back the message that she would be delighted to accommodate you. She has further expressed herself amenable to leaving at the hour of eleven."

"Eleven!" Damaris stuttered. "So soon..."

"You would have left even sooner had you remained with your original plans," Giles reminded her sweetly.

She flushed and looked down. "Where are we going?"

"To the Keep, of course. We're leaving so soon because I have hopes of arriving before nightfall. Consequently, I suggest that you repair to your room immediately and choose those garments that you will take with you for an extended stay in the country."

Damaris was visited by a whole spectrum of feelings. Out of these, indignation at so arbitrary a command as well as the enforced and unwelcome company of Cousin Phoebe moved her to cry, "I shan't go. I wish to leave with Mary!" She stamped her foot. "I will, too!"

"I must disagree with you, Damaris," Giles said coolly. "I have already given you my opinion on the subject of that arrangement. Certainly the happenings of last night have not altered it." His eyes grew even bolder. "On second thought, I expect you are packed, but possibly you might add some winter flannels."

"I . . . I hate you!" she sobbed.

His expression grew more taut and a strange expression—could it be pain?—flickered in his eyes. But he said simply, "It is your prerogative," and shrugged.

"I'll not go with you to the Keep," Damaris insisted. "You cannot force me to go."

"Ah." A mirthless little smile played about his lips. "There you are entirely wrong, my dear. If you do not consent to come with me peacefully, I will bind you hand and foot."

"You'd not dare!" Damaris gave him an outraged glare.

"On the contrary," Giles replied with a look that chilled her to the bone, "I suggest you do not challenge me on this matter. I cannot believe that you would like to have one of the footmen carry you to the coach."

"You . . . you are a monster!" she screamed.

"As I think I have mentioned, you are entitled to your opinion. Now do leave me and prepare for the journey."

Damaris had a horrid conviction that he meant exactly what he had said, and, weighing the matter, she decided to yield. It would hardly add to her consequence if a houseful of servants were to see her trussed hand and foot like a chicken ready for Mrs. Kimball's caldron. "Very well, Giles," she said with a coldness that, she hoped, surpassed his own. "I shall do as you say."

"I rather thought you would, my dear," he answered.

It was with extreme difficulty that Damaris refrained from slamming the door with a force that must surpass that used by Mary. He was probably expecting that and might even be disappointed at her restraint. She closed the door gently and went on up to her room. Once there, she found her anger suddenly and surprisingly dissipated. In its place was regret as she remembered the coldness of his eyes and voice. For the first time, she realized that she had sustained a significant loss. If Giles could not love her, at least he had been her friend. Now he was only her goaler.

CHAPTER
Six

THE SKY WAS a cerulean blue. There was a slight chill in the air, a reminder that September was gone and October a day old. But most of the trees in the large park surrounding Harwine Keep retained their vibrant green, Damaris noticed. She was in an ideal position to appreciate them, for, having been tossed by her horse into a bramble bush, her gaze was necessarily upward. She had been slightly shaken, but not hurt. In fact, her mood was one of annoyance because the brambles had caught her hair and habit at various points, and Gideon, the chestnut gelding she had been riding, was probably on his way back to his stall. She would need to walk back to the house.

Since she could not lie there for the rest of the afternoon, Damaris set about extricating herself from the bush, a process requiring patience and ensuring scratches as well as pulls at her hair. By the time she had freed herself from that thorny embrace, she had left strands of hair among its branches, her fingers were bleeding, and her annoyance had grown apace. Her habit had been ripped in several places, and that was a shame for it was very becoming and she doubted that any of the mantua makers in Wyke Champflower, the nearest village, were equal to the task of furnishing anything half so stylish! However, Cousin Phoebe, disagreeable though she was in most respects, was clever at sewing and mending. It was quite possible that she might be persuaded to give the habit her attention.

Oddly enough, Cousin Phoebe had not been as horrid as Damaris feared she might be given the tale of that aborted elopement. Though she had had quite a few words to say on the subject of ingratitude and propriety, she had also displayed an astonishing interest in the preparations for that night flight. She had gone as far as to admit, albeit grudgingly, that it was not mere vulgar curiosity that had prompted her questions, but rather a novel titled *Helena and Augustus*, recently published by the Minerva Press, which detailed just such an adventure.

"However," she had concluded, "'twas not the guardian who was in pursuit but the father, and fortunately they were able to elude him." She had paused, looking with confusion at Damaris, and then had added sharply, "But of course the situation was not at all the same. Augustus was not a reprehensible scamp. He truly loved Helena and eventually proved himself worthy of her by inheriting the fortune that had been stolen from him by a wicked uncle."

Later, it occurred to Damaris that she ought to have taken exception to Cousin Phoebe's dubbing Robert a "reprehensible scamp," but she had been so amazed by that lady's choice of reading matter that she had been rendered mute. Now, in the park, she could laugh at the incident. Yet even as she did she felt just a trifle guilty that she had not hastened to Robert's defense. Clandestine marriage or not, he could not be described in those terms. He was only a man deeply in love and just as deeply thwarted. One could only feel sorry for him, and Damaris did pity him. Pity, however, was several degrees away from the agony she should be experiencing.

She was sure that, if Helena had been separated from her lover by a cruel guardian, she would not have been reveling in such pleasures as the Keep and park had to offer. Until the branch had struck Gideon unexpectedly in the nose, causing him to rear, Damaris had been humming a waltz tune to herself. She feared it was the same melody to which she and said "cruel guardian" had danced at Almack's. Helena would have curled her lips in scorn at such a notion. She would have remained in her chamber, gazing out of the window and wondering where Augustus was. She might also have been sobbing and tearing her hair. Perhaps she would have rent her garments, a practice extremely popular in gothic novels. Helena would certainly not be speculating as to the feelings of her guardian toward herself—but stupid Helena did not have a guardian. A father was a far different matter than a guardian who was acting like a disapproving father. She sighed, then brightened. It did seem as if Giles's manner recently was not quite as frostbitten as on the morning he had banished her to the country. Though she could not describe his attitude as friendly, it was at least polite.

To do him credit, she must admit he had not referred to her projected elopement. He seemed to have put the episode out of his mind. She was only too happy to follow his lead. If she were entirely honest, she was very happy that matters had turned out as they had. She had not really wanted to marry Robert. If he had returned unscarred and with both eyes, she would not have thought twice about telling him the truth—or at least never have agreed to elope. At this moment, she could only look back on the earlier fateful evening with a shiver. She had spent many hours trying to convince herself that she was ecstatically happy, while deep inside she had been miserable. However, she was glad that Giles had shouldered responsibility for the ultimate outcome. She could not have hurt Robert, yet she could not help wondering if he would have been so considerate of her had the situation been reversed.

There was something cruel about Robert. That night he had come to her room and begun to make love to her, he had shown no regard for her feelings. He had stripped off her nightshift and afterwards . . . She blushed and winced at the pain he had inflicted in the name of love-making. Still, perhaps he had changed. His kiss had been more gentle. Who had taught him to be gentle? Was she being overly suspicious? She doubted it. She could not imagine a man of Robert's temperament and inclinations leading the life of a monk.

Damaris tensed. She heard hoofbeats on the path she had taken—the path that would eventually lead her to that crumbling Norman tower which gave the Keep its name. She moved into the shadow of the trees so as not to be in the way of the approaching horseman.

"Damaris . . . Damaris . . ."

Amazement flooded through her as she recognized Giles's voice. He had gone out some time ago to pay a visit on the vicar, but he must have returned. She was about to call out to him when he rode around the bend. She noted with a trace of satisfaction that he was looking extremely anxious. Hurriedly, she stepped away from the sheltering trees. "Giles," she said calmly.

His horse shook its head and snorted. Inadvertently, its rider must have jerked at the reins. Giles devoted scant moments to controlling the animal. Then, looking down at her, he said sharply, "You're here! Why did you come this far? What did you have in mind? Whom had you intended to meet?"

She blinked in amazement at his rapid series of questions and at the accusation in his eyes. "I do not understand," Damaris began in confusion.

"Why did you send your horse back to the stables?" he demanded.

"Send him back?" she repeated and then she understood his meaning. Anger replaced surprise. "Are you suggesting I had an assignation with Robert?"

"Your horse..." he began.

"I am glad he reached the stables," Damaris said in sugary tones. "When he... when I sent him back, I was not sure which direction he would decide to take." She managed a smile. "'Tis a pity you missed Robert—but, as you see, he too has gone. However, if you ride toward the village, I am sure you will be able to catch up with him. He neglected to tell me which hostelry has given him accommodation, but I presume it's the Lion and Unicorn, since that is the only respectable lodging to be had."

Giles bent down from his saddle to look at her more closely and then dismounted. Looping his reins around his hand, he came up to her. "Your cheek, it's bleeding," he said with concern.

"Robert's kisses, strong and passionate," she flared.

"And your habit's torn in several places."

"In the throes of violent passion. Robert is ever impulsive, as I need not tell *you*."

Suddenly Giles reached out a hand and pulled at her hair. As she jerked back indignantly, he said in a voice that was not quite steady, "And did Robert propose to weave a crown of brambles for your hair?"

"He..." Damaris paused, seeing that his lips were twitching. She could not restrain her own laughter. "No, actually, Gideon was startled by a falling branch and tossed me into a bramble bush. I thought I'd removed all of the briars."

Giles's incipient grin vanished swiftly. "You weren't hurt, I hope."

"No, it was an easy fall. Are you not ashamed of all your evil suspicions?"

He smiled. "I am. I expect I was relieved. I had been most concerned when 'twas reported to me that your horse had come back riderless to the stables. I thought you must have met with an accident."

"Which I did, O ye of little faith." She flushed as she remembered she had given him scant reason to trust her. "I have no intention of running away again, Giles."

His eyes softened. "I am glad of that. Robert is—"

Damaris raised her hand. "I want you to know that all that is at an end. I was very—"

Giles raised his own hand. "You need say no more," he interrupted. "I understand. My brother is very appealing, very charming, very persuasive, and he has suffered much. Yet I fear that even with all he has been through, he has yet to develop a sense of responsibility. When he does... But I think that will not happen immediately. He is very young yet. Meanwhile, you need"— he paused, his eyes on her face—"you need someone more mature, more considerate. It is to be hoped"—he hesitated again—"I hope you'll meet such a man."

Damaris found that she was holding her breath. A change seemed to have come over Giles. He was regarding her almost yearningly. As if... but no, she must be wrong. Giles could not care for her the way she had come to care for him. Not after all that had happened. She was indulging in the dangerous practice of wishful thinking.

"I must take you back to the house, my dear," Giles

said abruptly, "You'll be wanting a warm bath, else you'll be very sore tomorrow."

"I expect you're right." Damaris nodded, wishing she could say more, wishing she could tell him exactly why she had agreed to elope with Robert. Yet, if she did, what would his reaction be? She bit down a sigh. She could tell him nothing.

"Come." Giles lifted Damaris into the saddle and sprang up behind her, slipping an arm around her waist and urging his horse forward. He held her firmly. Her head was against his chest, and she could hear the steady beating of his heart beneath her ear. Did he need to hold her quite so tightly? She forbore to attach any special importance to that. Naturally, he had to hold her tightly; he had urged his horse into a canter. Soon they would be back at the stables and there would be no opportunity to voice the words hovering on her tongue. She must speak now.

"Giles..." she began tentatively.

"Yes?"

"I do hope we... we can be friends again."

His encircling arm grew tighter. "So do I, my dear."

"Then... then if we both wish it... are both agreed," she murmured, "surely..."

"You need say no more, Damaris. We are friends. In fact, I've never stopped being your friend. I expect I've seemed cruel and high-handed. Still, I hope you'll believe that I've only had your best interests at heart."

"Oh, I do believe that, Giles." She slipped her hand beneath the hand that clasped her waist and felt the pressure of his fingers hard against it. "May we consider that we have shaken hands on it, then?" she asked.

"We have," he agreed.

Was it merely by accident that he leaned forward so that his chin brushed against her curls? Probably. She did feel better though—much better. Though he had spoken as a guardian would speak, to have a guardian who was once more her friend was better than nothing.

Breathing hard, Damaris toiled up the grassy slope of the high hill known as Glastonbury Tor, toward the weathered old tower, all that remained of a fourteenth-century church. The greater part of it had been razed during that terrible time in the reign of Henry VIII known as the Dissolution of the Monasteries.

Damaris shuddered as she remembered that the last abbot of Glastonbury, the aged and gentle Layton, had, at orders from the crown, been hanged at the top of Glastonbury Tor. The spot had chosen so that one of his last sights in this world would be his beloved abbey, which had been once known as the holiest house in England, lying in ruins; its exquisite carvings, its noble arches, its beautiful cloisters, hacked to pieces by Thomas Cromwell's minions.

Though that tragedy had taken place some two hundred fifty years ago, the inhabitants of Glastonbury were wont to speak of it, as though it had occurred the day before yesterday. More than once a villager had indicated the hill and said to Damaris, "There be the place where the abbot were 'anged."

Determinedly, she shrugged this sad tale away into the past where it belonged. She was concerned with a much happier present. She was following Giles up that hill.

He was several yards ahead of her, which was slowing her progress because every so often she would stop and watch him. As she did, happiness stirred inside her. She felt it invade her whole body, had felt it ever since that morning at breakfast when he had said casually, "I am going to Glastonbury today, Damaris. Should you care to come with me?"

"Glastonbury? Oh, I should. I should like it above all things!"

"Good." He had smiled. "Then I think we might go within the hour."

Cousin Phoebe, who had been in the act of inserting a spoonful of gruel into her mouth, had set down her spoon and stared at them in querulous wonder. "Glastonbury. 'Tisn't much to see there save a lot of old ruins."

"But they're lovely," Damaris exclaimed. "And there's the Chalice Well, and the George and Pilgrim Inn, and the Holy Thorn tree . . ."

"That tree was cut down hundreds of years ago," Cousin Phoebe stated.

"But there are plantings of it all over the town," Damaris reminded her. "Poor tree. Imagine! It was supposed to have been planted by Joseph of Arimathea."

"Folderol! Papist lies, like all that nonsense about that cup."

"The cup?" Damaris repeated.

"That Our Savior was supposed to have drunk from at the Last Supper, the Holy Grail that was said to have been buried at the top of Glastonbury Tor," Cousin Phoebe said with all the scorn of a confirmed Methodist.

"Oh, Glastonbury Tor. I've always meant to climb that hill," Damaris said. "'Tis said you can see all England from its summit."

"Not quite all." Giles laughed

"Humph, by the time you've reached the top, you'll both be too tired to look," Cousin Phoebe remarked.

Now Damaris was tired but exhilarated. Giles had been different today. She had never seen him in such high spirits. It was as though he had shrugged off all the responsibilities of the estate and allowed himself to be completely carefree.

No, she was wrong—she had seen him in much the same mood. "The night of the ball!" she murmured to herself. Lord Harwine had given the ball. It had taken place in the immense ballroom at the Keep. She had been eleven at the time and forbidden to attend the festivities. However, she, Mary, and Robert had crept into the musicians' gallery, situated high above the floor and, fortunately for their purposes, no longer in use. There they had all lain flat on the floor peering through the rails of the balcony at the guests.

"There's old Giles," Robert had commented with a derisive grin.

"And there's his lady-love." Mary had giggled.

Damaris had followed Mary's pointing finger. Giles and Lady Laura were standing at the edge of the dance floor. Giles was wearing a green satin coat with a fall of fine lace at his throat. He looked amazingly handsome to her, even though he was yet the "enemy" in those days. Lady Laura, holding his arm and laughing, had been dressed all in white, a clinging silken gown cut very low across her breasts. There had been a diamond tiara in her golden curls and, though it was not the fashion, she had put a little black beauty patch at the corner of her mouth. They had both seemed so ecstatically happy that Damaris had been angered at Robert's sneering, "The moon-calf and his cow."

Then Damaris remembered something else—a much less pleasant vision. Giles was in the stables, grim-faced, red-eyed, surrendering his horse to the groom. The man was muttering something inarticulate and shaking his head. Lord Harwine had galloped up in a cloud of dust, dismounting swiftly, coming to Giles, and putting an arm around his shoulders. She had heard Giles say brokenly, "I begged Laura not to . . . to take that fence . . . 'twas too high, but . . . but she'd not listen."

"I know, my boy, but take comfort in the fact that death came quickly."

"Comfort . . ." Giles had echoed. "There's precious little comfort in that."

Damaris had crept away, fearful that he might see her

and think she had eavesdropped out of idle curiosity. She had not. She had heard the news of the accident brought by one of the hunters come back to fetch a doctor. She had hurried to the stables to find out if any of the grooms had returned. They would have told her what had happened.

She unleashed a tremulous sigh. Poor Lady Laura, dead at eighteen, and Giles's life blighted.

His mother had not thought so, Damaris recalled. "'Twas her own fault," Lady Harwine had said crossly. "Laura was ever a willful, headstrong creature. I am sorry for my poor boy, but I cannot help but feel him well out of such a match!"

Giles had not agreed. He had gone away after the funeral, returning months later, more quiet and aloof than before. It was then that he began to take more interest in the Harwine holdings. Even at twenty-two, he had proved to be a very capable administrator. Lord Harwine had often remarked on his ability. He had also expressed the hope that Giles would find someone to replace Lady Laura in his heart, but that had not happened. Damaris wondered if he still grieved for that golden girl.

"Damaris."

She started and found Giles at her side. "But you were so near to the top of the hill!"

"And, looking back, I saw you. I'd forgotten you were unused to such a climb." He slipped an arm around her waist. "You'd best let me help you the rest of the way."

She was about to tell him that she needed no assistance but his arm was around her—not a lover's clasp to be sure, but *there*. She let her shoulders sag slightly and dared to lean against him, though not heavily. "I am a little tired," she said. "The backs of my legs are pulling."

"Mine, too," he admitted with a smile. "That always happens on these steep grades, but you'll find the view worth every twinge."

The shade of Lady Laura dissolved like morning dew before the reality of Giles walking at her side as they neared the summit of the tor. She wished she had not come so far up that incline, for in a regrettably short time they had reached their goal and his arm had dropped. Moving ahead of her, he said, "Come over here." He took off his coat and spread it on the grass. "We can sit here."

"Oh, lovely!" Damaris exclaimed. Joining him, she fell silent as she looked out on masses of trees, on sunlit streams, and on the undulating sweep of moorlands which seemed to fall into the distant sea, its waters turned golden under the sun.

"Over to the east is Avalon." Giles pointed.

"Where they took the dying Arthur and the three queens," Damaris said dreamily. "And that stream over there, that might be the one where Sir Bedivere threw Excalibur and the Lady of the Lake received it."

"You seem well versed in Arthurian lore." He smiled.

"Oh, yes, I have read all about King Arthur. I wonder if he really did exist."

"His tomb was discovered on the abbey grounds," Giles reminded her with a twinkle in his eye.

"And I expect your father told you, as he did me, that 'twas considered politic by King Edward I that the monks find those bones, which might not have belonged to Arthur."

"He told me, but it was a while before I believed him. As a lad, I spent a great deal of time searching the abbey grounds, hoping to find a spearhead or a rusty lance, some relic of those chivalrous days that had been over looked by all the thousands of people who came here through the centuries." He laughed. "I need not tell you that I was unsuccessful."

"I did not know you were interested in King Arthur, too!"

"How could you know?" he demanded. "I was 'the enemy.'"

Damaris stared at him, wide-eyed. "You knew we called you that?"

The teasing smile that curled his lips brought Robert to her mind, but she quickly dismissed him as Giles said, "How could I not know? I had eyes and ears."

"You always seemed so . . . disdainful."

The smile left his eyes. "Did I? I expect I was a bit shy."

Damaris had an instant vision of a boy standing on the stairs watching her, a tentative smile on his face. She had started toward him, only to have Mary grab her arm. "Do not go near him. He's horrid."

"Why is he horrid?"

"Because he is," Robert had chimed in. "He's the heir and thinks himself better than the rest of us."

Damaris suddenly realized that Robert had been burning with jealousy. She realized, too, that he was still jealous. "Oh, dear!" She looked down, running her hands through the grass. "I do wish I'd known you wanted to be friends."

"Well, we are friends now, are we not?"

She kept her eyes on the grass. "You have much to forgive me, I fear."

"No."

It would have been wonderful if she had dared to tell him the truth. "I was so foolish," she said instead.

"All of us have been similarly foolish, Damaris," he replied seriously. "All of us have thought we loved . . . and have been mistaken."

Was he referring to Lady Laura? Had he come to realize the folly of being headstrong, daring, and heedless? She looked up, but failed to catch his eye. He was gazing moodily into the distance. Then, as if aware of her gaze, he turned back to her.

"So much folly." He sighed.

He was putting her thoughts into words. "But not everything," she said softly.

"No." He was silent, looking at her. Finally, he said, "You are very lovely. In fact, every day you seem to grow more beautiful. I am thinking..." He paused and sighed.

"Yes?" she breathed.

"I am thinking that when we return to London, I shall be kept very busy."

"In what way?"

"Being your guardian."

"Oh." She was so disappointed that she was hard put to keep the tears from her eyes. She had believed that for a moment—but it was no matter what she had believed. She managed to say lightly, "I shall do my very best to make your tasks as easy as possible."

"How will you do that, pray?"

"I shan't be over-encouraging." She smiled up at him. "That should keep your audiences with prospective suitors to a minimum."

"You cannot tell what you will do. You've had little opportunity to know anyone, save Robert and myself," he said regretfully. "But that night at Almack's, seeing you so surrounded, I had a taste of what my future would be."

"Oh," Damaris said disdainfully, "most of them were so silly. I've forgotten all their names—all save one."

"And who was that?" Giles demanded quickly, his eyes intent.

She longed to point at him and say, "you," but what would have been the use of that? She shrugged and sighed. "Alas, his name has also escaped me."

"I am sure he's not forgotten yours, my dear."

She laughed lightly. "'Tis a pity we cannot wager on it. He is a man who could have his choice of females, and, most probably, he does."

"Were you so taken with him, then?" Giles demanded with a small frown.

"I did find him mightily attractive, but we had only a single waltz and then he left me for another . . . lady and another and another. So you see . . ." She shrugged and laughed.

"A veritable bee among the flowers," he observed dryly.

"An admirable description."

"I'd not have you fly with bees."

"Why not?" She gave him a challenging look.

"Because, my dear, they have stings. I should not like you to be hurt."

"Alas, even a guardian cannot prevent that," Damaris murmured.

"He can try." Giles gave her a long look. "And *will* try. You know, Damaris, it is my earnest desire that you be . . . happy." His eyes seemed to burn into hers.

She returned his look with one of equal intensity. "I am grateful for that, Giles. But even you cannot carry happiness in your pocket."

"I wish I might."

"And I wish I might have some for you," she dared to say.

"You do."

Her heart was beating heavily. It was a wonder he could not see its movements. She said on a breath, "How might that be?"

"You . . ." he began, then paused, adding with a friendly smile, "you have made this day very enjoyable." He rose swiftly. "Now that we've rested, let us do some more exploring. Should you care to go up in the tower, or would you prefer to go down to the abbey?"

Again she was very aware of something left unsaid. More than that, she was certain that this time she had surprised a look of yearning in his eyes. In that moment, she was sure—nearly sure—that he did care for her. Yet why would he not speak? And then she thought she knew. Robert still stood between them. She must prove to Giles that she cared for Robert only as a brother. It would take time, but she had plenty of that. They would be remaining at the Keep for most of the winter. "I think I should prefer to go to the abbey," she said.

"Good. And afterward I imagine we'd be better for a light collation at the George and Pilgrim."

"But do you not have matters to which you must see in town? Isn't that why you came?"

"No, I came only to visit Glastonbury. I thought you might be glad of a change from the Keep—and from Cousin Phoebe as well."

"Oh!" Damaris exclaimed. "How very kind of you." Impulsively, she stretched out a hand to him. Grasping it, he pulled her to her feet and, picking up his coat, slung it over his shoulders.

"'Twas my pleasure, my dear."

"And mine."

Again he turned from her, saying, "You must be careful in walking down the hill. You could easily slip on the grass and fall."

Damaris laughed. "There was a time when I should have run down it!"

"But not today," he cautioned seriously.

"No, not today, since I must obey my guardian."

"Who wants only to keep you from all harm, Damaris."

"I know, I do know, Giles." She gazed up at him, wanting to add "darling" Giles, "dearest" Giles, Giles, "my love," but such endearments must wait, too.

Taking his proffered arm, she walked sedately by his side.

CHAPTER
Seven

"BUT I DO not understand." Damaris stood in the small octagonal chamber that served as the breakfast room at the Keep. She was staring perplexedly at Cousin Phoebe.

"No more do I." That lady shrugged as she buttered a scone. "Best partake of the eggs. They are quite tolerable this morning. For once Mrs. Kimball took my advice and did not scramble them to a turn. The roast beef is uncommon juicy and tender, and the ham is especially tasty."

"I am not hungry," Damaris interrupted, as she stared at the place where Giles usually sat. "He said we were to go riding immediately after breakfast. When did he leave?"

"An hour since." Cousin Phoebe had a mildly curious expression on her face. "I'm told he was in a rare taking. Peake—"

"Peake!" Damaris echoed and sped from the room. She rushed up the stairs to Giles's chamber but did not find the valet there. He was probably in the servants' hall. Going down to that part of the house, she found him breakfasting and exchanging pleasantries with Sara. They broke off, looking surprised and not a little self-conscious as she came into the room. Both rose immediately.

"Peake," Damaris panted, "where is Lord Harwine?"

He shook his head. "I'd not be knowing that, Miss Damaris. A message came this morning, an' 'e left within the hour."

"He gave you no word of where he was bound?"

"None, miss."

"But that's so odd." An idea occurred to her. "He did not mention Mr. Robert?"

"No, miss. Just 'ad 'is 'orse saddled an' 'e were off."

"Thank you, Peake." Damaris proceeded to her chamber. She was extremely surprised; more than surprised, she was badly disappointed and perturbed. It was unlike Giles to leave so precipitously with no message for her, when yesterday he had most particularly asked if she would ride with him the following morning. She had assented immediately, and he had told her that they would go immediately after breakfast.

Damaris had been excited by the invitation. Generally, Giles hastened through breakfast and was off to confer with his estate agent or visit farms or oversee fields. But for the second day in a row he had expressed a preference to be with her! Surely that must mean something, expecially since the request had come at the end of a day spent entirely in her company, a day that would serve to enshrine Glastonbury in her heart forever and which had sent her to bed to dream of him.

Actually, she had dreamt of King Arthur and Sir Lancelot riding up Glastonbury Tor but with Giles's visage beneath their helmets and wearing that special look that had been on his face as he had bade her goodnight. Falling asleep, she had been considering that look, trying to understand why it was so different from all his other expressions. She had decided that happiness had wrought the difference. She had never seen his eyes so glowing and vibrant—not since the night of the ball with Lady Laura at his side. Was that ghost finally exorcised?

Damaris had risen this morning full of the hope that on this ride he would finally unburden himself—for it was very obvious to her that he wanted to tell her something. When they had supped at the George and Pilgrim, he had looked at her so—dared she call it "lovingly"? No, why should he love her? She was really building air castles. Lofty ones! Yet, he *had* wanted to ride with her and... where had he gone? It was very confusing. It was also alarming. What had happened? Who had sent him that message and what information had it contained?

Again Robert was in her mind. Was that the answer? Had he gotten into another scrape? It was not unlikely, and, though Giles had, in effect, disowned him, that would never keep him from rushing to his aid were he in real difficulties. That must be it. Damaris could not imagine anything else that would send him forth without a word. She felt a little more cheerful. Of course, she was concerned about Robert, but mixed with the concern was a larger resentment. It gave the lie to his earnest protestations that he had changed and become more responsible. Yet, he had not changed—his proposing of that hole-in-the-corner wedding was much in keeping with the old Robert. Of course, it had been Mary's idea— but he had agreed to it immediately, saying that he could not have thought of a better solution. He and Mary had laughed at her protests. Damaris shuddered. If it had not been for Giles's timely intervention, she would be wed to Robert and her life quite ruined. She had really been very foolish. Pity was no surrogate for love. Every hour she spent in Giles's company made her more thankful that he had saved her from a most unhappy existence.

"Dearest Giles," she whispered. "Do hurry back." She sighed and went to change into a morning gown.

"Miss Damaris . . . oh, Miss Damaris."

She was seated in the little folly at the end of the garden, where she had been reading a short article entitled *Singular customs at Arracan, in India Beyond the Ganges,* which had appeared in last August's issue of *La Belle Assemblée.* Though it was most informative on the subject of medical practices in those hot regions, it had failed to hold her interest. Now she looked up to find Sara hurrying toward her, a look of mingled surprise and alarm on her face. Unconsciously, Damaris's hand stole to her throat, where her pulse had quickened.

"What is it, Sara?" she asked nervously.

"Oh, m-miss, you must come. There be a lady wot's just arrived."

"A lady," Damaris said with some relief. Nothing had happened to Giles, then.

"Yes." Sara nodded. "An' Miss 'Averstoke says I must find you. Oh, I am that glad I did."

"What lady? Who is she?"

"Oh, miss, 'tis passing strange an' Peake, 'e be dumbfounded."

"Why would that be, Sara? Who is this lady?"

"Oh, miss, she says she be the Viscountess Croy."

The journal fell from Damaris's fingers. Jumping up, she gasped. "She says . . . what?"

"She says as 'ow she's the Viscountess Croy, 'n she's that sorry that the master be gone. She says as 'ow she sent a message that she was at the Golden Cock on the 'igh road, 'n' she'd like it if 'e'd meet her, but then she decided to come the rest of the way because she couldn't wait to see 'im 'n' the 'ouse 'n' all. Oh, miss, an' 'e . . . 'e never said nothin' to nobody."

"It cannot be," Damaris said numbly, but she remembered the message that had come that morning. Cousin Phoebe had told her that she had heard Giles was in a "rare taking," which was not unnatural in the circumstances.

But Giles couldn't be married. It wouldn't be like him to keep his family in ignorance of a wife. There must be some mistake. "Where is she, Sara?" Damaris asked.

"She be in the drawin' room, 'n' she's brought ever so much luggage wi' 'er, an'—"

Sara broke off as Damaris hurried up the path toward the house. Reaching the garden door, she stopped to catch her breath, but though she succeeded in that endeavor, there was nothing she could do to quell the tumultuous pounding of her heart. "There must be some mistake," she whispered. "'Tis not like Giles to . . . no, I cannot believe it. He is too honorable. He would never . . . no, he would never." Having assured herself again that a man of his integrity would not—could not—keep so momentous an event as his marriage from his family, Damaris grew much calmer and was, in fact, in total command of herself by the time she had walked through the several state rooms that brought her to the drawing room. Approaching the door, she found it ajar and consequently heard the lady's voice before she saw her.

In tones that were high and sweet, the new arrival was saying, "Oh, dear, I do wish I'd not said I'd await him at the inn. 'Twas foolish of me to have done so, though I expect 'twas even more foolish to have come ahead. It's a marvel our ways didn't cross, or perhaps he took a different route. I . . . I presume there are many roads to Rome." A nervous laugh followed this artless speech.

Taking a deep breath, Damaris opened the door wide

and came to a dead stop at the threshold, staring at a tall, blond young woman who was modishly dressed in a blue traveling ensemble.

"Ah, Damaris, my dear," Cousin Phoebe said gratefully, looking unusually distracted. "I am glad Sara was able to find you."

The young woman turned swiftly. She was wearing a close-fitting bonnet with a small veil that did nothing to disguise the fact that her eyes were huge and blue, that she had a straight little nose, and a lovely mouth— that, in fact, she was a beauty. Her loveliness, coupled with a slim, willowy shape, awakened Damaris's memories of Lady Laura. She was much like her, save that those huge eyes were not full of laughter. In fact, they had hardened perceptibly as Damaris entered, and they had also given her a look that started at her head, swept to her toes, and rose again to fasten on her face.

Damaris, meanwhile, had clutched at the doorknob behind her. There was a ringing in her ears and a buzzing in her head. She felt perilously close to swooning, but she must not. She said weakly, "I have been told that—"

"Oh." The visitor produced a smile that did not rise as far as her eyes. "You are Damaris Vardon, no doubt? My husband gave me a most accurate description of you, I see."

"Indeed?" Damaris managed to say.

"Oh, yes, he said you'd lived with the family for a long time, even though you are not a blood relation."

"Yes." Damaris nodded, not trusting herself to say more, even though a dozen questions were crowding to the tip of her tongue. She wondered if she were not perilously close to hysteria.

"He has told me so much about you all," the woman who must be Lady Harwine was continuing. "And about the house. I had no difficulty in recognizing it. Such a beautiful old place, though 'tis a pity the castle crumbled. I do love castles. Oh, dear, I wish he were here. I am so longing to see him."

"I expect he must . . . must be equally anxious to see you," Damaris said.

"Is he well?" Her blue eyes were suddenly anxious.

"Oh, yes, he is in excellent health."

"Ah, I am relieved. I know there's been much to trouble him with his brother and all. He did say I should wait until he sent for me, but 'tis so long since we've been together, and, when I received his last letter, I decided I would wait no longer."

"I quite understand." Damaris nodded.

"I . . . er . . . think the Blue Suite must be readied for . . . ah . . . Lady Harwine," Cousin Phoebe suggested, her eyes darting from one young woman to the other.

"Is that where my husband sleeps?" Lady Harwine demanded.

"No," Damaris said, "but it is very comfortable and—"

"I shall stay with him. He would prefer it so. 'Tis how it has always been."

"Very well." Damaris endeavored to produce a smile, but failed. Her face felt frozen. She turned to Cousin Phoebe. "You will see that Lady Harwine is made comfortable."

"Oh, I shall see to that myself," the new viscountess asserted. "You need only send the housekeeper to me."

"The . . . housekeeper?" Cousin Phoebe repeated blankly.

"Yes." Lady Harwine favored her with a chill smile. "I should not presume upon either of you ladies to attend to my comfort. Rather, it must be the other way around, I'm thinking."

"You will excuse me, then, I hope," Damaris said through stiff lips.

"Oh, yes, but do come back. Perhaps when I am settled in, you'll tell me all about my new domain so that I may surprise his lordship with my knowledge."

"I should be delighted," Damaris murmured.

A few moments later, standing in her chamber, Damaris stared about her blankly. She could not remember having climbed the stairs, but she was breathing hard which suggested that she must have dashed up them. She put her hands against her head. Questions were speeding through her brain. How . . . where . . . when? But she could not think clearly—not until she was away, far, far away. She pulled at the bell rope and then again.

"I'm 'ere, Miss Damaris," Sara said behind her.

Damaris jumped and whirled about, "How did you . . ."

"I been 'ere, miss," Sara explained. Her eyes were round with curiosity. "Miss, is she—I mean she cannot be . . ."

Tears clouded Damaris' eyes. She blinked them away furiously. "Yes, she is. And I beg that you will pack for me, Sara."

"P-Pack, miss?"

"Immediately. I am going to Taunton. The coach to London will stop there. I . . . I am going to Lady Mary."

"Will you be tellin' old Linch to ready the post-chaise, Miss Damaris?"

"Yes. No! I shall ride."

"Alone, Miss Damaris? Ye cannot go alone," Sara said in shocked tones. "Not on the stage. Let me come wi' you. Your 'orse'll bear the two o' us."

There was good sense in that suggestion, and Damaris did need to think sensibly and as coolly as possible. Sara must be instructed to say nothing to anyone in the servants' hall. By the time the abigail had left the room, she had been sworn to secrecy and instructed to be ready within the hour. Once she was alone, it struck Damaris that Sara had appeared singularly unsurprised by that sudden decision, which suggested to Damaris that her feelings about Giles were known. Had he known them, too? Had he taken her to Glastonbury in order to tell her about this dreadful, forward, managing creature, who was already acting as if she were the lady of the house? But did she not have every right? She was Giles's *wife*.

Damaris moaned, feeling a pain in the region of her heart. Tears poured down her cheeks, and she blinked them back. She had to think. No, she had to ready herself for the journey. She could not just stand there like a statue. Yet, why had he not told her yesterday? Had he, divining her feelings, been unable to frame that expla-nation? Had he intended to tell her this morning? Suddenly his odd mood on the hill became clear.

"So much is folly," he had said, looking so moody.

That woman had muttered something about his in-structing her to wait until he sent for her. There was the suggestion that he had not wanted to send for her—and why not? She was quite lovely, and she did resemble Lady Laura.

Perhaps that was it. She had looked like his lost love, and he had made the mistake of thinking she was another Lady Laura. Damaris snapped her fingers. That *must* be it! He had been bemused by that similarity, and on an impulse, he had wed her and deserted her. Deserted her? Giles? Damaris could hardly believe that and besides, she did not act like a deserted wife. He must have visited her from time to time. And . . . Damaris found she was crying again. Again she brushed the tears away. Giles was not worth them, he who had concealed his marriage for so long.

Now many of his actions were explained. All those trips to the country, whilst they had been living in Lon-don. He had told her, and she had believed him, that they were on behalf of his tenantry. Instead, he must have been visiting *her*. It was all too terrible, too demeaning to realize that she..."I must get away," Damaris said aloud.

It was fortunate that she had some money though it was a great pity she could not control her fortune. She did have her mother's jewels. She could sell them and might need to do just that, for, in this moment, she had come to another decision. She would not stop long with Mary; she would go farther yet. At last there would be nothing to keep her from returning to her own estate in Northumberland!

"Giles is wed," Mary said incredulously. "Wed? Giles?"

Damaris nodded, disliking Mary's stunned reaction even more than the giggles she had anticipated. At least when Mary giggled, she did not talk, did not keep repeating a fact over and over again until it had worn grooves in Damaris's ears!

"And you actually spoke to the creature?" Mary demanded.

"I have told you I did. I have told you the whole of it." Damaris released a weary sigh.

"And she is the image of Laura?" Mary shook her head. "That goose."

Damaris brightened briefly. "Was she?"

"Most assuredly. Those who knew Lady Laura told me she hadn't a particle of sense, which was probably why Giles admired her."

It was on the tip of Damaris's tongue to tell Mary that she had never understood or appreciated her elder brother. Unfortunately, and all too quickly, she remembered the agonies and the trials of the last twenty-four hours, most of which had been spent on the coach from Taunton. To one unused to such exigencies, it had been a frightful experience. Damaris had been wedged in beside Sara, all too aware of the far-too-friendly glances or, rather,

leers of a plump gentleman who reeked of violet scent.
At every bump in the road, and there were many, he had
contrived to put a plump hand on some part of her anat-
omy—this despite her abigail's loud and angry re-
monstrances. He had also tried to accost them at the
coaching inn, where they had been obliged to spend the
night. He had not been discouraged by the broad hints
of a slammed door and furniture wedged against it. He
had been equally obnoxious during the rest of the journey
and revoltingly presumptuous upon reaching London.
Fortunately, a friendly stranger, who was truly friendly
and had no ulterior motives, had routed their tormentor
with the threat of fisticuffs and called them a hackney.
Damaris had arrived at the house in Park Place feeling
wilted, dirty, and dispirited and all because of her married
guardian, Giles Harwine, who did not deserve to be de-
fended! All of these thoughts flashed through her mind
in an instant and in answer to Mary's slander, she said
tartly, "Very likely!"

"Well." Mary took a turn around the half-furnished
drawing room. "I shall be glad to put you up here, my
dear, but"—she rolled her eyes and looked exceedingly
self-conscious—"you ... ah ... came at a ... very difficult time, and you've not given me an opportunity to
tell you about poor Robert."

"*Poor* Robert," Damaris echoed. "Is anything amiss
with him?"

"Everything." Mary groaned. "You'll not credit this,
my love, but 'tis true. Robert has been clapped into the
Fleet! 'Tis the most outrageous thing, and I unable
to—"

"The Fleet!" Damaris interrupted. "You'll not be telling me he's in debtor's prison?"

"'Tis exactly what I am telling you, my love." Mary
groaned again and made a gesture as if to run her hands
through her beautifully coiffed locks, but, evidently

thinking better of it, she forbore to disturb the hairdresser's art and contented herself with wringing her hands. "Oh, I am at my wit's end, trying to beg or borrow the money to free him! 'Twas all the fault of his horrid landlord and his tailor. Oh, yes, and the bootmaker. Really, I do not know what tradesmen are coming to. In Papa's time, they never insisted upon being *paid,* though Papa did pay then, as you know. But poor Robert could not—and he didn't owe them more than a month. But word spreads so *quickly*.

"The fact that he lost twenty thousand pounds on a turn of the cards at White's became common knowledge overnight, and all those wretched creatures appeared immediately to dun him. He was half-foxed and could not elude them and was dragged off to the magistrate, who read him a horrid lecture on the evils of gambling. He said he would make an example of poor Robert, and now Robert is in this dreadful cell, and I cannot apply to Giles, and Robert tells me he is beginning to loathe the very sight of a racquet."

"A racquet?" Damaris repeated confusedly.

"Well, I have been able to give him enough money to buy him a room by himself in the rules—you know, that is away from the middle of the prison—but I had to furnish some security to the warden for his debt to the amount of three percent of what is owed. It comes to fifteen pounds a week, my dear. 'Tis all I can manage. So much of my money is tied up in funds, though Bannerston's been able to help out, too. But neither of us can produce the five thousand pounds needed to free him. I had been thinking of lowering myself and writing to Giles, but now with this creature installed... Poor Robert, my heart bleeds for him each time I visit him. His only exercise is playing tennis, for of course he cannot get out and the room he occupies is horrid. 'Tis a dog's life. If Robert had not been away so long, the tradesmen would have known what to expect, and he might have been able to apply to a friend. But he is out of touch with all his old comrades. I suggested going to the commander of his regiment, but he absolutely forbade it. And the mercenary little wretch with whom he had been living..." Mary broke off, looking distressed. "I am sorry, my love, I did not mean..."

"No matter, I am heart-whole," Damaris assured her mendaciously. "Robert has found himself a *chère amie,* then?"

"There is naught that is *chère* about her," Mary said bitterly. "She'll not lift a finger to help him for all the feathers he has left in her nest—jewels, a carriage. Bannerston quite agrees with me that she should be whipped at cart's tail like the common little lightskirt she is. But 'tis all the same with opera dancers."

As Mary came to a stop, Damaris, plucking the wheat from the chaff, asked, "Is Bannerston your adviser, then?"

Mary flushed and said defensively, "Well, I was monstrously lonely, and I have known him for years. He is charming, and if he were free, we should be wed. He has said so. Also, he has been so helpful in finding me workmen to effect alterations in this house, and Lady Bannerston remains in the country—a confirmed invalid, my dear. She never rises from her sofa, and what could be more natural for a gentleman who is not yet thirty-nine and a dear friend of poor Francis, really very close... and so ardent and... You'll look down your nose, I am sure, but, you see, 'twould have been better if you... But no matter, I shall give you accommodation, poor child. Imagine Giles being married! It is too strange by half!"

Again Damaris was able to sift through Mary's disjointed speech for the kernel of matter it contained. "Is Bannerston living here, then?" she demanded bluntly.

Mary took a backward step, and her eyebrows shot

toward her hairline. "My dear, what a suggestion! I do hope I have not given you the impression...No, certainly not. He resides at his lodgings in Jermyn Street, the most discreet of men, but I...I never know when he'll take it into his head to...pay me a visit...sometimes after White's. So you see," she finished vaguely.

"I do, my dear, but I've not come to stay more than a night and a day. I am going on to my home—"

"*Your* home?"

"'Tis near Hexham in Northumberland."

"Oh, yes." Mary clapped her hands. "I remember hearing about it from Papa. Such a splendid notion, my love."

"Yes, I knew you must agree," Damaris said dryly.

Another flush bloomed on Mary's cheeks. "My dear Damaris, as I once told you, I would be...or would have been most happy to have you with me, but with Giles being so adamant and you being gone near six weeks and..."

"My dear Mary, I do not want to remain in London. I am longing to see my old home. I can scarce remember it. But, meanwhile Robert cannot remain in the Fleet!"

"'Tis all very well for you to say that, but I tell you, I've not the money."

"I have some of my mother's jewelry with me," Damaris interrupted.

"Her jewelry? Surely you cannot mean—"

"But I do. There are gold bracelets and a ruby pendant and a tiara of diamonds and pearls. I will show you the lot."

"But Damaris, my dear, they must be heirlooms and as such...well, you will marry and..."

"They are not heirlooms," Damaris said, resisting the temptation to add that she would never marry—not now. She continued, "These were purchased new and given to my Mama by my father. There are some heirlooms as

well but they, like my fortune, are available to me only
at the discretion of my guardian."

"Giles," Mary muttered with a grimace. "And I am
sure they will remain unavailable. We can hope only that
his new wife will not take a fancy to them."

Damaris glared at her. "Giles would never give them
to her. He is an honorable man."

"I cannot think he has acted very honorably in this
regard," Mary returned.

"Doubtless he had his reasons."

"How quick you are to fly to his defense," Mary
marveled.

"Fair is fair," Damaris retorted. "Now, as to the jewels, I must have funds to travel north, so I have brought
them with me with intentions of selling them. I am sure
we shall be able to realize enough for both our needs."

"Oh, Damaris, my dear," Mary breathed. "And you
have called yourself heart-whole."

Damaris frowned. "If you imagine that I still have a
tendre for Robert, let me assure you that 'tis quite the
contrary. I am entirely convinced that we should never
have suited."

"Dear," Mary said regretfully, "I wish I had not mentioned that horrid opera dancer. But I assure you 'twas
nothing, my love. Gentlemen have *needs*, but I know,
for a fact, that Robert's feelings for you remain unchanged."

Damaris was annoyed at Mary's arch look. She opened
her mouth and closed it on further protests. It did not
matter what Mary believed or did not believe. Her reasons for wanting to free Robert from durance vile did
not arise from what she had once termed her love for
him. They were based on the debt of gratitude she owed
to his parents, who had brought her into their home and
treated her as considerately, as kindly, and as warmly as
if she had been one of their own children. With that in

mind, she could hardly let their beloved son languish in the Fleet.

There was also another reason, and that was the affection she still retained for her old playmate. But, as she would have told Mary, had she been willing to listen, affection was quite different from love. To Damaris's everlasting sorrow, she now knew that the latter emotion carried with it an intensity of feeling which was quite foreign to anything she had ever experienced before, and she was drearily certain that she would never know its like again.

CHAPTER
Eight

THE SKIES WERE lowering and gray. A blustery wind tore
at Damaris's skirts as the footman assisted her from the
hackney, which she had hired at the Green Gauntlet on
the high road. Standing nearby, Sara shivered and pulled
her woolen cloak tight about her shoulders. Damaris followed her example. She felt very cold. However, she
attributed that chill as much to the great gray house that
loomed over the semicircular driveway as to the inclement weather. Even if it had been as sunny as it had been
five days earlier, when they had begun this journey, she
doubted she would have found that house to her liking.
Though it resembled the sketch in her room at the Keep,
it seemed to her that it had not appeared as fortresslike
as it did now, an effect that was accentuated by its cas-
tellated roof.

Memory had also obiterated its color. She had not expected it to be so gray. And even though the grounds were well tended, there was something singularly unwelcoming about the place. Certainly it formed a far from agreeable contrast to the mellow golden walls of Harwine Keep. To look at Vardon Hall was to remember the old days of the Border Wars and the bands of marauding Scots who were wont to stream down from the Lowlands to burn, pillage, rape, and steal livestock in retaliation for English forays into Scottish territory.

Looking up at that facade, Damaris thought that its windows seemed like so many dark eyes staring blankly into the distance, oblivious of her. She was loath to approach its heavy oaken door, which, she noted, was centered with a massive brass knocker in the shape of a dragon. However, she could not remain there with the footman wanting to deposit the luggage and the coachman eager to be paid and sent on his way.

Moving forward, Damaris caught the dragon around its scaly middle and shivered at the coldness of the metal that pierced even her glove. Drawing it back, she slammed it against the plate. It fell with a loud clang, and, at the same time, a gust of wind hit her with a force that nearly toppled her. She clutched at the doorknob, wondering if there was anyone within that vast pile to hear her summons. She had sent a message ahead, but had the caretaker received it? At that moment, she nearly fell forward as the door was swung back on to reveal a well of darkness behind it.

"Ach, thee are here already," someone remarked in a cheerful voice with a heavy northern accent. A small, plump woman clad in a neat gray gown stepped over the threshold and looked curiously at Damaris. "Ach," she repeated with a wide, welcoming smile that revealed two deep dimples in her apple-red, apple-hard cheeks. "Coom in, coom in, 'tis blowin' a gale an' there's the smell o' rain in the air. 'Tis a pity, for yesterday 'twere bright as a new-minted sovereign an' me hopin' 'twould be thus when tha got here." She held up a candle, peered closer at Damaris and, sucking in a breath, let it out in a gasp of amazement. "Ach, an' doesn't tha have the look of herself that hangs in the gallery. I thought it might be so. I saw tha when tha wast a little thing, no higher than so." She stretched out her plump hands. "Thy hair was as black as thy een, 'n' as dark as her that sailed wi' Queen Catherine."

"My ancestress," Damaris breathed.

"Aye, the Portugee. An' a stir she made coomin' here wi' her foreign ways an' her strange, uncouth songs. 'Twas many hereabouts thought she'd bewitched the master, an' said 'twere a blessin' she died bearin' her first son. But coom in, coom in. I should not be keepin' you a-talkin' here an' the wind tearin' at tha and thy girl. Ach, an tha has luggage, does tha not. Rafe!" She glanced over her shoulder. "Rafe," she called again.

"Aye, missus," a voice responded in the darkness behind her.

"See to the luggage, lad."

"I must pay the driver," Damaris said quickly, reaching into her reticule and producing some coins.

"Bless ye, gi' the money to Rafe. He'll do that." The woman smiled as a tall, lanky boy with a cap of unruly red hair came forward to stare owlishly at Damaris out of large rust-brown eyes.

"Aye, I'll do 't, missus." He stretched forth a huge hand and, taking the money from Damaris, added, "Tha'd best get close to yon fire."

Damaris smiled up at him. "Thank you, we shall." She waved to Sara, and they both hurried into a paneled hall, which was dark by reason of the small, set high windows that allowed only slivers of light to filter inside. A single candle in a brass holder stood on a table near a steep flight of stairs. Its flame, unsteady in the draft, did little to brighten what appeared to be an immense space. The hall was permeated with the smell of beeswax and dampness, the former probably hastily applied on the furniture once her message had been received. There was no sign of the fire Rafe had mentioned, but at least there was no wind, either.

Damaris turned to the woman, "Are you the caretaker, then?"

"Bless thee, I'm not. I be his daughter-in-law. He's at the house 'cross the park, toastin' his bones. He's got the rheumatics. Come fall he's as stiff as a board wi' em. I'm Mrs. Proctor 'n I'm to gi' thee his greetin's. We're both that glad tha's coom. 'Tis a long time since a Vardon's set foot in here. But I do remember your mother and father. My own Ma were employed here when they was alive." She shook her head. "Such a shame as 'twas. They was both such kindly folk. An' I'm that glad I can do for ye until others coom from the village. Shall tha' be stayin'?"

"For the nonce." Damaris gave an uncertain look at the cavernous hall. The ceiling was lost in darkness, and the sense of familiarity she had hoped to experience had not yet emerged. But she was curious about that "Portugee" who hung in the gallery.

Harwine Keep had a gallery with portraits dating back to the fifteenth century. Thinking about them, and about the way the features of Giles, Mary, Robert, and Deborah appeared on one or another face throughout the centuries, Damaris realized that she had been so long a part of her adopted family that she had given scant thought to her own. It was an oversight that must be remedied. Possibly it would serve to take her mind off her troubles. It might also make her feel less displaced. Until that moment, she had been regretting the impulse that had borne her northward. During the greater part of her journey, she had fretted over leaving London. However, in addition to not feeling welcome at the mansion in Park Place, she had not wanted to see Robert, had, in fact, insisted on leaving the city before Mary and Lord Bannerston arranged his release from the Fleet. To have seen him again would only have intensified her longing for his perfidious brother, whom she was doing her best to hate—but alas, with scant success. Furthermore, she feared that Robert, aware of her aid in purchasing his freedom, might think her as much enamored of him as before, which would have been extremely awkward.

"Where be the fire?" Sara asked through chattering teeth.

Damaris threw her an apologetic glance. "Oh, yes, we must find that fire. I am sorry to have kept you standing for such a long time, Sara."

"'Tis naught, Miss Damaris," Sara said with equal haste.

"Ah, you're chilled, lass?" Mrs. Proctor nodded. "'Tis a cold day. I'll give thee some hot tea an' a bit o' spirits in it." Taking the candle from the table, she moved toward the stairs. "The fire be up here. Thee'll need to hold tight to the banisters. 'Tis dark on the stairs an' they be steep. I'll be leadin' the way."

The stairs were not only steep, but they also seemed to disappear into darkness. Though the candle afforded some light, its flame sent distorted shadows to dancing on the walls. Gazing at them, Damaris was reminded of the Border Brownies, small stunted creatures that came to help with the household work when the servants were abed. Swarthy and misshapen, they disappeared before morning. Who had told her about them, Damaris wondered. It had been here in this very house. Her old nurse, no doubt. She smiled, glad of the memory, wanting more to come.

"Now," Mrs. Proctor said as they reached the upper

hall, "I've put thee in the guest chambers on t'other side of the saloon. The upstairs where thy family used to sleep be all closed off. I've given thee a corner chamber an' there be a small room next door for thy girl. 'Tis cozy there. An' this'll be havin' the mornin' sun, which'll be makin' it a sight more cheerful."

It needed to be more cheerful, Damaris thought a few minutes later, as she stood in the middle of the designated room, looking at walls covered with faded paper and patched with dampness in some areas. But, the furniture had been polished recently, and the large four-poster bed was hung with flowered chintz curtains, which appeared to be new. At least one note of cheer was added by leaping roaring fires in both her room and the one allotted to Sara.

"Should tha be wantin' that tea? I'll be after fetchin' it for the now," Mrs. Proctor offered.

"Oh." Damaris glanced at Sara's white face and stiffly held body. "We should. That would be very kind of you."

"I'll not be long." Mrs. Proctor bustled out of the room. With her, Damaris thought, went some of its cheer.

"You'll need to take off your wraps, Miss Damaris," Sara said as she divested herself of her own cloak. "'Tis warm in 'ere."

"Yes, it is becoming so, isn't it?" Damaris remarked thankfully. Unbuttoning her coat, she surrendered it to Sara, then glanced around the room again, still bemused by the unfamiliarity of her surroundings. She was also more than a little daunted by the fact that she would be in charge of this immense establishment.

And there would not only be the house to think about. It occurred to her that there were also tenant farmers. And had there not been a large dairy? She could not think of these responsibilities now, but they would need her eventual consideration.

She had an instant memory of Giles's supervision of

his own far-flung properties. But she must remember that not all the time that he had absented himself from London or from the Keep had been spent in overseeing his holdings. There had been the surrogate Lady Laura. And where had he found her? Now that Damaris thought of it, she realized that the new viscountess had an odd accent. That was not to say that her voice was not cultivated, but there was an intonation. But Damaris did not want to think of *her*.

She found Sara still standing in the middle of the room, looking as if she were having a prolonged attack of the dismals. She was still wearing her bonnet and cloak, and, to Damaris's dismay, she looked as if she were about to snatch up her discarded cloak, wrap it around her, stalk out the door, and take the next conveyance back to London.

"Sara, dear," Damaris said, "'twas a long ride, and you do look sadly weary. Why don't you rest. I know you found it hard going in the coach. I'll have Mrs. Proctor bring your tea and a warming pan for your bed."

Sara turned a surprised and disapproving face in Damaris's direction. "Oooh, I couldn't do that, miss. 'Oo'd see to the unpackin'?"

"I'll see to it," Damaris assured her.

"But that wouldn't be right, Miss Damaris. An' besides, there's naught that's wrong with me. It . . . it just takes a while gettin' to know a new place." Sara suddenly sniffled and threw her hand up against her eyes.

"A place that isn't London or anywhere that you know." Damaris put an arm around Sara's shoulders. "I know it must be strange to you—strange and frightening. And you are tired and have, I know, slept badly of late. I want you to go to your own room and get into bed. You'll feel much the better for a nap."

It took considerable persuasion before the girl would agree to do her mistress's bidding, but finally she curtsied and went into her own chamber.

Damaris breathed a sigh of relief as the door closed. If Sara had a good sleep, it might serve to put her in a better frame of mind. However, it was obvious that the girl disliked this part of the country. She had been getting gloomier and gloomier the farther they had advanced. Suddenly Damaris realized that there might be other reasons for the abigail's distress. A vision of a blushing Sara and a teasing Peake came to her. Peake was a nice-looking man. Yet wasn't he a little old for Sara? No, he could not be out of his twenties. Damaris had never considered that aspect of the situation—and should have before so summarily uprooting the girl. She had not considered anything or anybody save her own woes. She had just taken the abigail for granted.

But Sara was not merely an object to be transported back and forth at will. She was much of her own age and very pretty. Was she also in love, and had she experienced heart wrenchings similar to Damaris's own when she was forced to leave the Keep? Was she even now sobbing into her pillow because she feared she would never see Peake again? That must not happen. Once she herself was acclimated, she would send Sara back to London on some pretext or other.

Damaris swallowed a large lump in her throat. When Sara went, she would be quite alone, and alone she would remain. She did not expect to have visitors here. Though she had had to inform Mary of her ultimate destination, she had exacted a solemn promise from her not to reveal it to either of her brothers. That, of course, would pose some problems since Damaris would be needing funds— but not yet. The jewelry had fetched a much better price than she had anticipated, enough to free Robert and provide her with sufficient monies for now. Later she *would* need to deal with Giles.

For perhaps the hundredth time since she had left

London, Damaris wondered how he had reacted to the news of her disappearance. Had he been concerned? More likely he had been angry. He might even have felt betrayed since she had, after all, promised she would never run away again. However, if he had any imagination at all, he would understand why she had broken that particular promise. Actually, she would have preferred it if he had not understood: but the more she thought about it, the more she was convinced that he had guessed her reasons for making it in the first place, guessed that she cared for him. Her fists knotted, and she frowned. Why was she still thinking about this man, who was now so many leagues away, dallying with his lovely new bride?

But his bride was not new!

Only Damaris's knowledge of her existence was new. She had asked herself a question, and she could provide a most adequate answer. She was thinking of Giles because, at present, she had little else to occupy her mind. Tomorrow would be a different matter. Tomorrow she would begin setting her house in order, and if all the walls were in such disrepair as those in this chamber, she would have more than enough to claim her attention.

The anticipated rain had come in the night, and past two o'clock in the afternoon it showed no signs of abating. Great billowing clouds hung over wind-lashed trees, and occasionally the skies were seared by jagged slashes of lightning, followed by horrendous crashes of thunder.

Though Damaris had never feared such heavenly wrath, she found the resulting dimness depressing. Furthermore, Sara had caught an eye-watering, nose-reddening case of the sniffles, which served to dampen her spirits still more. Though Sara had come in dutifully to help her dress, Damaris had ordered her back to her room immediately. She had gone more sulkily than gratefully. Later, she had protested vociferously when Damaris had brought her tea and toast.

"'Tis not ye should be doin' for me," she had snuffled. "An' I should've 'elped ye wi' your dressin'."

Rather than being cheered by Damaris's assurances that she had managed that feat very well by herself, Sara had turned weepy, expressing the fear of being turned off without a character. This sentiment had left her mistress sorry that Sara's state of health was giving rise to these baseless fears, but pleased that her abigail had no intention of leaving her service, Peake notwithstanding. Still, Damaris wished that the girl was not feeling so poorly. She would have liked her company. She would have asked Mrs. Proctor to come with her to explore the house, but immediately after providing a midday meal for her, that kind woman had begged to be excused that she might tend her aged father-in-law.

"I be the only one t'home. My husband's ridden off across the Border 'n the old one'll not be able to fetch his dinner less 'n I'm there. Rafe is somewheres about. I'll have him build fires in the hall an' thy chambers. An' I'll be back to gi' tha a bit o' supper," she had said, adding anxiously, "That is, if 'tis thy pleasure that I go."

Naturally Damaris had accorded her the necessary permission, but the great house seemed very empty without Mrs. Proctor's cheerful presence. If she had remained, perhaps Damaris would not be feeling so depressed. The sensation was augmented by growing fear that, in returning to her home, she had acted far too precipitously.

Unfortunately, there was little she could do about that now. As her old Nanny had been fond of remarking, she had made her bed. "And there'll be no turning back now," she muttered aloud. It was not precisely the saying—but it would suffice.

Still, there was the portrait gallery to visit as well as the other rooms in the house. There was also the possibility that she might remember things about them that would serve to make the Hall seem more like her home.

That, she realized now, was the greatest disappointment. In coming here, she had hoped to resurrect memories of her parents and some few scenes of her childhood; but save for such images as already lingered in her mind, these were proving extremely elusive.

Because of the prevailing darkness, Damaris had brought a candle to light her way through the passages. As she turned into a narrow corridor, she saw a pair of doors to her left. A tendril of memory stirred. She had the impression that such doors opened onto the gallery. But as she put her hand on a knob, she realized her destination lay further along that same corridor. Thrusting the candle into the dark room, she glimpsed book-lined walls. The library! She moved back, as pleased by her recognition of her error as if she had found the room itself.

"'Tis farther along *this* corridor," she whispered. "I am almost sure of it." Moving forward she passed the stairs and paused again. Raising her candle, she found another pair of doors a few feet ahead of her. "There," she murmured triumphantly. She pulled open the door to her left and blinked against light that streamed through a series of windows, each wider than any she had seen in the other rooms. Coming inside, she blinked away sudden tears. She had not been mistaken! The walls about her were covered with paintings!

"The lady . . . I want to see the lady," a tiny voice in the back of her mind whispered, a voice out of the past.

Damaris set her candle down on a table near the doors and walked toward a huge marble fireplace. Standing in front of it, she looked up and again there was a voice in her head—a lovely, musical voice.

"Look, look, my darling. There is Maria Elena, who was lady-in-waiting to Catherine of Braganza, who married Charles II. Lift her up, Rom, that she may see."

A deeper voice—a man's voice—agreed excitedly,

"Yes, yes, and you are right, Melissa. She is Maria to the life!"

"Mawia," a tiny Damaris, held in strong arms, had lisped.

No one needed to lift her now as she gazed into the huge brown eyes of a slender, dark-haired, golden-skinned beauty in a rose-colored gown edged around the low neck with pear-shaped pearls. Matching pearls hung in her ears, and a necklace of large round pearls adorned her throat. She held a guitar.

Tears stood in Damaris's eyes. She did recognize the portrait. She also recognized the white marble mantelpiece held up by a pair of caryatids, one on either side of the immense fireplace. Similarly familiar were the soft faded reds, blues, and golds of the Aubusson carpet that stretched the length of the huge room. For the first time, she felt she had indeed come home!

The feeling grew more intense as she wandered from portrait to portrait. Small flashes of memory sped across her brain as rapidly as the lightning streaked the storm-troubled thunderheads beyond the windows. Stopping before a painting of a dark man in a gold and scarlet doublet, his narrow face framed by a stiff lace collar, his short hair half hidden by a black velvet hat adorned with rows of rubbies and a single feathery plume rising from an onyx buckle, she knew without looking at the plaque on the lower part of the frame that this was Sir Christopher Vardon. He had been briefly the beloved of Queen Elizabeth, until Her Majesty learned that his wife was pregnant! He had been sentenced summarily to the Tower on a trumped-up charge.

Her parents had never told her this tale directly but she, following after them as they walked through the gallery, must have heard them discussing it. The dates of the portrait proved her right. He had been born in 1552 and died in 1587, never knowing that he had a son,

Sir Thomas Vardon, whose grandson, back from exile in Holland during the days when the Puritans occupied the Hall, had married Maria Elena, the Portuguese "witch" who had played on her guitar and sung strange songs.

There was another beautiful lady, her hair dressed high over a cushion and lightly powdered, though one curl descended artlessly over her bare shoulder. Her name was Belinda Belmonte. She had married a long-faced gentleman in a powdered wig.

"Beautiful, Belinda Belmonte," someone had remarked teasingly. That alliterative phrase rose from the depths of Damaris's memory.

"She was beautiful, Melissa." Those words had been spoken defensively.

"And a shocking flirt—even now, when she is full of years. And jealous of your wife."

"Melissa, you are speaking of my mother!"

"Indeed, yes! And what, I wonder, does she say about me?"

Damaris searched among the portraits. Suddenly she found what she had been seeking: the full length portrait of a girl in a flowing white gown, her fair hair dressed à la Grecque. Damaris's eyes blurred as she looked on the face that also smiled from her locket. The eyes staring back at her were unnaturally solemn. As Damaris remembered them, those eyes had never been solemn; they had been full of laughter. Melissa had even made her dignified husband laugh. He had been painted in a dark blue jacket, white vest, and white breeches. He was clasping a tricorne.

"Why did you wear your hat, Romulus? You were not outside."

"'Twas to give me something to do with my hands."

"I've never known you to have any difficulty in finding something to do with your hands, my love. At least not when you're with me."

"Melissa! You are quite outrageous."

"I do hope so, dearest Rom."

Damaris laughed and was startled by the sound as it echoed through the huge chamber. A moment later her eyes were wet again and, moving closer to the two portraits, she stretched out her arms to them. "I do wish I'd known you," she whispered. "Indeed, I could almost wish there were such things as ghosts."

"Do not wish that, my angel, lest you be visited by Beautiful Belinda Belmonte—and she was a perfect horror!" She could imagine her irrepressible mother cautioning her and could also imagine her father's scolding following fast upon it. But how he must have loved her!

"They was clasped in each other's arms when they was found on the shore."

Where had she heard that? No one had told her that her parents were dead—not even Lord Harwine when he came to fetch her—but she did remember that her nurse had been given to weeping overmuch in the days before he arrived.

Damaris swallowed a lump in her throat as she remembered herself asking, "What do you mean, Nanny?"

"Ach, little pitchers have big ears. Never tha mind, child. I meant nothing."

Damaris pressed her hands to her ears. The room seemed full of voices. She looked toward the doors— but no, she did not want to leave just yet! She retreated to a long piece of furniture swathed in dustcovers. Upon removing the cover, she found it to be a gold-framed chaise longue with gryphon legs and two gryphon heads at its back. It was covered in blue and white striped satin. Damaris could imagine her mother stretched out upon it, her fair curls spread over the bolster. She, herself, sat on the floor and ran an experimental finger into the open mouths of the gryphons.

"'Tis passing hard," her mother had complained. *"But 'tis monstrous stylish."*

"'Tis passing hideous," had been her father's com-

ment. *"I've little use for chairs with crocodile heads and tables with claws."*

Moving to sit down on the chaise longue, Damaris agreed that it was hard. Still, it was with a marvelous sense of continuity that she, too, stretched out upon it, putting her head on its small bolster and looking up at the carved plaster ceiling. Yet, as she lay there, she shivered and glanced at the empty fireplace. Memory supplied orange flames feeding on huge logs. In her parent's day, there had been fires in all the rooms. She was sure of that. She remembered liveried servants, pokers in hand, stoking them and sending showers of starlike sparks traveling up the chimney. The house had had a huge staff of servants who had worn green and blue livery. She had a fleeting memory of a table heavy with silver and crystal on a fine damask cloth and her mother in a diaphanous blue gown coming into the dining room. At least fifty guests must have been seated with a footman in a powdered wig standing behind each chair.

Damaris shivered again. She must find Rafe and have him build a fire. Where had he gone? Mrs. Proctor had not told her, but she had indicated that he was someplace about. She should have demanded that the woman be more specific. The reins of the household were in her hands, but she had yet to control this mettlesome and mighty steed. She would begin in a small way by fetching Rafe.

She went to pick up her candle. To her dismay, it had burned down to a tiny pinpoint of flame ready to be drowned in the melting wax. She glanced around the room. There were candelabra on the mantlepiece, but the holders were empty. She hoped she could traverse the corridor before the flame was extinguished.

Damaris hurried into the hall, but scarcely had she taken a few steps when the flame sizzled out, leaving her in darkness. She moved to the wall and groped her way along it. A few minutes later, she saw a wavering light ahead of her. Quickening her pace, she came to the head of the stairs. As she had suspected, the light was coming from the entrance hall, where a fire had been built in the huge stone fireplace set into the far wall. Looking down, she caught the gleam of metal in the curve of the stairs. Unbidden, a name sprang to her lips.

"Sir Hugo!" she whispered with delight and ran lightly down to the ground floor to confront a suit of armor—or, as her nursemaid had called it, "the metal man." She had made up a bit of doggerel about it—"Metal man, metal man, catch me if you can."

Riding into battle astride his armored charger, Sir Hugo Vardon had caught quite a few unfortunate Scots, impaling them on his lance, which was now set into the wooden platform at his feet and seemingly clutched in his empty metal gauntlet.

"Metal man, metal man," Damaris whispered as she looked up at his visor. She remembered childish dreams in which he had chased her through the park. And had King Arthur's knights worn similar armor as they jousted in the courtyards outside Glastonbury's castles? No. Sir Hugo had fought under Henry III. By then King Arthur was long dead if, indeed, he had ever existed, and Glastonbury was leagues and leagues from Northumberland, and Giles was probably walking in its meadows with his new bride!

"And may the snows come early and last through April!" Damaris whispered and shuddered, remembering that ill wishes come back to plague their sender.

Scarcely had this thought crossed her mind than she was startled by the brassy clang of the knocker hitting its plate with considerable force. She hurried to the door. Undoubtedly Mrs. Proctor or Rafe had returned. She had opened it before remembering that neither would have entered through the front of the house. In that same moment, she was caught and held tightly in a damp embrace while a well-remembered voice said brokenly, "Oh, my dearest, my very dearest, why did you run away from me?"

CHAPTER
Nine

"ROBERT!" DAMARIS WHISPERED, when at length he released her.

"The same, my own darling," he murmured, closing the door and standing with his back to it.

Her lips felt bruised, and she was half-suffocated from pressure of his arms. She wished fervently that she had never opened the door to him—to Robert, whom she had not seen since the night of that aborted elopement; Robert, whom she had once believed she loved and who now stood looking at her with a mixture of tenderness and surprise. Angry words piled upon her tongue. Mary had betrayed her! But she was not surprised. After all, Mary adored Robert. She probably still hoped he would marry Damaris.

"Come in," Damaris said.

Robert laughed tenderly. "But I am in, my dearest, dearest Damaris."

"Yes, so you are." She managed a smile. "I . . . I did not expect you . . . you would have come this long way."

His face was a study in conflicting emotions. Surprise, concern, hurt and even anger radiated from him. "Did you imagine I would not?" he cried passionately. "Do you not realize that I would have followed you to the ends of the earth to express my gratitude and my love." He caught her by the shoulders, his fingers digging painfully into her flesh. "Lord, if you knew the torment I have endured, prisoned in that hell, cut off from you, with no ray of hope to lighten my gloom. Then of a sudden Mary and Bannerston—who had both been full of polite and empty regrets at their inability to extricate me from my troubles—came to free me. When I would have thanked them, they told me 'twas you who were my benefactor! You, my blessed angel, whom I thought never to see again!"

Damaris would have preferred it if he had been a little less extravagant in his gratitude. She would have preferred it if he had not been there at all. Unfortunately, he *was* there and she must be gracious. "I am glad I was able to help you," she said, "but . . ." She paused, seeing for the first time that his hair was plastered against his forehead and that his coat was running water. "But Robert, you are very wet. Come, you must stand by the fire!"

He lost no time in obeying her. "I thank you. Come stand with me," he said, edging as close as possible to that blaze. "It's cold in this house, and what a storm is raging. There was such thunder and lightning that more than once I thought my horse would throw me."

"You rode here on horseback?"

"The inn had no hackney to provide."

"Why did you not wait until the storm subsided?"

"Do storms ever subside in this benighted district?"

He smiled but sobered quickly. "I could not wait—not when I had come so far and knew you to be so near." His mouth twisted. "Oh, Damaris, why did you leave without a word for me?"

Damaris's indignation at Mary's betrayal of her confidence increased. She did not know what to say. None of her explanations would really suffice save that truth which, out of kindness, she was loath to express. "I . . . I was on my way north," she said, "I had bought passage on a stagecoach and—"

"That's no excuse," Robert interrupted, adding sharply, "Why do you not tell me the real reasons behind your actions?"

Damaris tensed. Robert did not lack perception, and dissembling had never come easy to her. Even so, she was reluctant to divulge her real feelings. She said uncomfortably, "I do not understand you."

"I am of the opinion that you understand me all too well," he retorted. "Why do you not say that you have come to hold me in abhorrence because I lost so much at the tables."

Damaris breathed easier. "It was not that—"

"I say it was," he said shortly. "And also 'twas your fault!"

"Mine!" she exclaimed. "You blame—"

"No," he interrupted quickly. "I have no blame for you." He seized her hands. "My dearest, I beg you to believe me when I tell you I was beside myself with agony that night, wandering around in a veritable daze of pain."

"You were ill. Your wounds . . ."

"No. Can you not understand what I mean?"

Damaris tried without success to free her hands from his viselike grip. "No . . . I . . ."

"Very well, I was ill, if you like, sick at heart over our separation. Imagine my sensations on the night when, returning to the house, I was confronted not with my beloved little bride, but with Giles. God, if you could have heard his laughter. It yet rings in my ears."

"Giles laughed? Why?"

Finally Robert dropped her hands and moved back. "He laughed because of my confusion at the trick he'd played on us, and then he turned uglier still—as he derided my feelings for you and sneered at what he termed my 'pretensions.' I went down on my knees to him. I begged him to reconsider, but he was adamant. He said if I dared seek you out, he'd have his servants thrust me from the door—thrust me from my home, Damaris, as if I were some villainous intruder! I care not if he is the heir. I grew up on our estates. I love the town house. I love every blade of grass at the Keep. But 'twas not the loss of my home that mattered. It was you. Without you, my dearest darling, life ceased to have any meaning for me. Consequently that night at the tables, I did not know what I was doing. I was nearly out of my head with melancholy."

He sounded compellingly sincere. Nonetheless, Damaris would have found that anguished explanation easier to accept had Mary not informed her of his opera dancer. However, since it would have served no purpose to mention the dancer, she said, "I am sorry." She broke off as Rafe strode into the hall. The boy's mouth dropped open when he saw Robert.

"Oh, Rafe," she said quickly, thankfully, "would you build a fire in the gallery. I think my guest and I would be more comfortable there."

"Yes, missus," he mumbled, his owlish gaze shifting from Robert's face to her own, "I'll be fetchin' some wood, missus." He bobbed his head and went out.

"Good God!" Robert exclaimed. "Who is that lout? The village idiot?"

His scornful query annoyed her. Suddenly she had a

feeling of oneness with the past. The Vardons of Vardon Hall had always championed and protected those who wore their livery. Though Rafe did not go clad in blue and green, he, too, was her responsibility. "He's not in the least simple," she said firmly, "He was probably surprised to see you here. He helps Mrs. Proctor with the work. She's the daughter-in-law of the caretaker."

"There are only two servants in this vast pile?" Robert asked incredulously.

"There's Sara, but she's abed with a cold. And of course there will be more. I arrived only yesterday, you see."

"And have it in mind to remain here?"

"It is my home." Damaris threw a proprietory glance at the suit of armor. "It has been the home of the Vardon family for hundreds of years."

"What will Giles have to say about that? But you've run away from him, have you not? From both of us, in truth."

Damaris drew herself up. "I've not run from either of you. I have only decided to return to my home. 'Tis time. Indeed, 'tis past time."

"Possibly, but I cannot see your guardian agreeing with that. He gave me to understand that there were five years remaining of his golden rule."

"I cannot believe he would want me at the Keep now."

Robert's laugh raised echoes throughout the hall. "Nor I." His mirth vanished abruptly. "That unmitigated hypocrite. To call me down for what he termed a 'clandestine marriage'! And all the time secretly wed himself."

Again Damaris was prompted to defend Giles, but what could she say? Robert had spoken no more than the truth. Giles was, indeed, a hypocrite. "It's very strange," she said sadly.

"No, perhaps 'tis not so strange," Robert mused.

"Though my worthy brother's never been known to be a gambler, he might be playing a deeper game than any to be found at the tables in Whites or Watier's. And—" He broke off, frowning as Rafe, his arms full of logs and kindling, stumped up the stairs.

Damaris waited until the boy's heavy footsteps retreated down the upstairs corridor. Then she asked, "What are you hinting, Robert?"

"My love, I am hinting at nothing. I am about to divulge my opinion—or, if you like, my theory concerning this most enthralling subject. Now, it did seem to me when I had my last confrontation with my beloved brother that he spoke not only as your guardian, but also as one who had a far more lively interest in his little ward."

"No," Damaris contradicted. "You cannot be hinting—"

Robert raised his hand. "Softly, my dear. I have already told you that I hint at nothing. I beg you will possess your lovely little soul in patience. On the night when he came bristling and snarling at me like any manger dog, I was quite certain that he wanted you for himself."

Damaris felt a flush mount her cheeks and a sharp pain pierce her heart. "That is absurd!" she exclaimed. "He has no love for me."

Robert took a turn around the hall and returned to stand close beside Damaris. He smiled down at her. "I quite agree. I acquit him of wearing his heart on his sleeve. Rather, I should think 'twas in his purse or, rather, your reticule . . . and 'twas because he has a hand on those strings that he wants you to be secured."

A most unwelcome suspicion stirred at the back of Damaris's mind. She longed to put it from her but could not. In a low voice she said, "You'd not be suggesting . . ."

"What am I not suggesting?" he demanded. "No matter, I'll not require you to provide the answer to what we both already know. Now." He began to pace back and forth again, shooting sharp glances at her as he did. "From what you've told Mary, his bride's appearance was unplanned and unexpected?"

"So it seemed to me." Damaris's hands knotted into fists at her sides a second time. If Mary had been present, she would not have hesitated to box both her ears or, better yet, put a bridle on that babbling tongue, as used to be done with common scolds and gossips!

"Then I put it to you, Damaris. He must have wanted his lady to remain away until the time was right—and that would be when he'd laid seige to your heart and—"

"Giles never—" she began.

"Heed me," Robert interrupted. "Giles is clever and patient. These two attributes are common and most necessary to gamesters. I, alas, possess neither virtue, if so they can be termed. Now, having disposed of me, as he believed, could he not have played upon your affections and—"

"But he did not!" Damaris flushed, remembering how much she had craved that very thing.

"Hold, my love. I have said he was patient and did not realize that his bride might prove impatient. Consequently, he settled for proximity, remaining with you in the country, seeing you every day. Might he not in time have grown more gentle, more cajoling, hoping to win your regard and, having done so, might he not have either seduced you or—"

"No!" Damaris interrupted. "He would not . . . could not."

"But he was not to know that," Robert reminded her softly.

"He—"

"I beg you to let me finish, my dear. You may disagree

with my theory or, in fact, agree with it. I pray only that
you let me continue."

Her curiosity being equal to her anger, she gave a
short nod. "Very well."

"I thank you, Damaris. And having won your heart
and something equally precious, could Giles have not
placed you in a position so untenable that you would be
happy to buy his silence?"

"No, no, no!" she cried. Before she could say more
about what she could only term as "invention" better
suited to a work for the popular theater, Rafe came down
the stairs.

"I beg pardon, missus. The fire be set in the gallery
'n' candles in yon sconces to light the way."

"Thank you, Rafe. 'Twas most considerate of you."

The boy gave her a shy grin and, bobbing his head,
hurried out of the room.

"'Twas not considerate, my dear," Robert muttered.
"'Twas no more than his duty."

"Possibly, but the poor lad's got so many duties,"
Damaris replied.

"Why else is he here? But I should not dare give you
instructions on how to manage servants. 'Tis your house
after all. The gallery, I hope, has more comforts than
this drafty hall?"

"It has," Damaris assured him. She was glad to be
diverted from an argument which, rather than rousing
her suspicions of Giles, was forcing her to defend him—
which, in her present state of mind, she was most un-
willing to do. It would be far more to her taste to show
Robert her newfound family.

The fire had caught quickly, and the chill was gone
from the chamber. Damaris stood beside Robert as he
gazed up at the portrait of Maria Elena. "Are we not
very much alike?" she asked.

"Amazingly so." He looked at her, then back to the

portrait. "But I believe her descendant surpasses her in beauty."

Damaris flushed. "I fear you are teasing me."

"On the contrary, I was never more honest. My vision has not suffered greatly from my loss," he added quickly, as if fearing she must believe he was seeking sympathy. "Tell me, are the stories I have heard about her true?"

"The stories? I cannot believe she was a witch, if that is what you mean."

"A witch? I never heard that." He smiled. "I did hear that she defied the wishes of Queen Catherine and His Majesty, the scapegrace Charles, who had an eye on her, and fled the court with her lover, who was your ancestor."

"Yes, I believe she did." Damaris nodded.

"And..." He stared at her. "Perhaps I do credit that other tale, as well."

"The other tale?"

"That she was a witch. For surely you've cast a spell on me."

Damaris moved away from him. His eyes had grown intent and uncommonly bright and hard. He reminded her of a predatory bird about to descend upon its prey, but immediately as that conceit crossed her mind, she dismissed it. This was Robert, *Robbie*, her old friend, the favored playmate of her childhood, the man she once believed she had loved. "Now you are really teasing me," she said lightly.

"On the contrary, my love, I was never more serious. Why do you think I followed you across half of England?" He moved to her side and, turning to face her, put his hands on her shoulders. "Answer me, Imp."

"I...I did not mean that you should," she faltered. "I told Mary..."

"Why did you not mean it?" he demanded.

She tried to move away from him, but he did not relax his grip. "Robert, please," she began.

"Please, what?" he rasped. "You've been acting very peculiarly for a female who, but a few short weeks ago, stood ready to fly with me to Gretna Green. What has changed you?"

"I am not changed," Damaris began, only to be silenced by his kiss.

Lifting his head, he said jubilantly, "Are you not, my love? Then we must finish what we began. I want you. I need you and, by God, I shall have you."

Damaris heard him in a daze. Once more her lips were bruised by the force of his hard kiss, but she could not fault him for his breach of conduct. She had invited it, assuring him that she had not changed. In effect, she had meant that she had never loved him, and she would have amplified her statement had she been given a chance. She had forgotten how very impulsive Robert could be. Now it was imperative that she tell him the truth she had longed to spare him.

She searched his face.

Evidently his weeks in the Fleet had wrought heavily upon him. He looked thinner, almost haggard, and there was a driven, desperate quality in his tone and gaze that she did not fully understand. Tentatively, she said, "You forget, Robert, that Giles is still my guardian."

His laughter was loud and unexpectedly harsh. "But Giles, my love, is at the Keep, cuddling his new bride. And we are here, and Scotland's not a day's journey hence. You'd not thought of that, had you? If I remain here this night, we can be gone at dawn. No need to dash to Gretna Green. All that's required anywhere in Scotland is a declaration of intention to be wed—with witnesses to hear it—and we'll be joined in bonds that cannot be severed, not even by your determined guardian."

Robert's grasp had loosened, and Damaris was able to move away from him. Stepping back, she said decisively, "No, I'll not be wed in such a manner."

"Why not, Damaris?"

He was frowning now. He looked almost menacing, and Damaris wished fervently that she had not let him know there was such a dearth of servants in the house. She was aware of a craven desire to flee the chamber, but as she glanced at the door, she met the concentrated gaze of those centuries of pictured Vardons. She drew herself up. She could not shame their memories by turning tail and running like a scared rabbit. She was not Giles Harwine's orphaned ward, nor need she be intimidated by his brother! She said coldly, "It is not fitting that a Vardon of Vardon Hall lend herself to this hole-in-the-corner proceeding."

"This hole-in-the-corner proceeding?" Robert echoed incredulously. "You were willing enough before." He glared at her, and it seemed to her that his scar had deepened in color, reflecting his anger. "You've changed your mind, have you? You've decided you no longer love me. That's the real reason behind all this procrastination!"

He had arrived at that conclusion with very little prompting from herself. She was glad of that, but still she needed to be gentle in her answer. "I've not stopped loving you, Robert," she began.

"Then, why—" He took a step forward.

Damaris put out her hand. "Hear me, I beg you. I have always loved you as a brother but because I was young and silly and because you were going off to war, I thought...but I was mistaken. I think I knew that before you returned and—"

"Damn you!" he cried furiously. "Your actions belied your words. You *did* love me and love me still." He moved close to her and clutched her shoulders, shaking her. "But for some mad reason of your own, you are determined to play this...this game of hare-and-hounds with me. I'll not allow it, do you hear? We're past these subterfuges. You'll wed me, Damaris. You must."

She was caught between fear and surprise. That desperate quality in him was more evident than before, and his face was so distorted by fury as to be hardly recognizable. It was also far from loverlike. Indeed, he did not seem at all like the Robert she had known. Possibly, that was due to his anger. She discovered that she was angry, too. That emotion rose to a peak as she retorted, "I shall do nothing of the kind, Robert. As I told you before, I'll not wed you, not ever. Now, please let me go."

His eye was blazing. His lips had writhed into a snarl, and his scar flamed blood-red against his white face. His fingers, talonlike, pressed into her flesh. "Very well, you misbegotten little wretch. As it happens, I've no real desire to wed you or bed you, either. But I am deuced short of the ready, and, since you are a 'Vardon of Vardon Hall' and should like to hold your head high in this particular part of England, I have a bargain to propose."

"A bargain?" Fear rose in her now, but she would not let him see it. "You want me to give you more money?" she added contemptuously. "Is that it, Robert?"

"Aye, much more, my dearest love. Do they not say in the Bible that the price of a virtuous woman is above rubies, or some such thing? What price do you lay on your virtue, my sweet Damaris? Mind you, I do not ask for rubies. I'll settle for gold, and if I do not receive it, my dear love, your depleted staff will find me in your bed. Think how this tidbit will titillate your neighbors."

He appeared half-mad. His eye was boring into her. He looked as if he could strangle her but, of course, he would do nothing of the kind. He wanted her money, had always craved it, she suddenly realized.

Something else occurred to her: his theories concerning Giles's fell schemes. He had reeled them off so very glibly, suggesting that they had not been invented on the spur of the moment, suggesting that they had long been in his mind. Again she remembered the way the viscountess had spoken, the hard *r* that did not sound even English. Thoughtfully and, considering her present perilous situation, Damaris said, "That woman who came to the Keep had so strange an accent."

His cruel grasp grew even harder. "What are you talking about, damn you? What is Giles's doxy to us? Do you not understand what I am telling you?"

"Yes, I understand perfectly. You are saying you'll ravish me if I do not give you money," Damaris returned contemptuously. "In effect, you are doing exactly what you accused your brother of contemplating. That woman who claimed to be Viscountess Harwine may well be *your* bride, Robert."

"What are you saying?" he rasped. "You cannot believe—"

"Oh, yes, I do believe it," she cried. "If I'd not rushed away so impulsively, I am sure that poor girl would have revealed all. She is very tall, Robert, very fair with huge blue eyes. She looks more than a little like Lady Laura." She saw him turn from white to red, saw his eye look away from hers, and knew she had her answer. "Oh, Robert!" She shook her head. "How could you?"

His expression had turned ugly. "Very well, 'tis the truth, damn that blasted, importunate little jade. I am wed! But that particular truth'll not make you free. Only money can do that, and since my brother must yet control your fortune, you'll write to him and—" His grip suddenly went slack as a loud crack bearing a singular resemblance to a pistol shot rang through the room from the direction of the fireplace.

Damaris took advantage of the diversion made by the burning log and wrenched herself free of him, fleeing into the hall. He would be after her in a trice, but fortunately Rafe had lighted only those sconces leading to the gallery. The rest of the passageways lay in darkness. Damaris herself was confused momentarily, but in another instant, she had gotten her bearings. She dashed toward her chamber and hurried inside.

Tears were close. Ruthlessly, she held them back, ignoring the temptation to throw herself on her bed and sob her heart out. That would be useless. Robert might soon discover her location, and she would be a prisoner. It would not be hard for him to intimidate her servants. Flinging her cloak about her and grasping her reticule, she opened her door quietly. A moment later, she had slipped into Sara's room. The girl lay asleep but awakened immediately, her mouth opening as she saw Damaris at her side. Fearing an exclamation, Damaris put a finger to her lips, and, kneeling beside Sara's bed, whispered urgently, "Mr. Robert's here, and I must go to London."

"With 'im?" the abigail squeaked.

"No, he mustn't know I've gone. As for you, 'tis best—"

"I'll go with you, Miss Damaris," Sara interrupted, slipping out of bed, revealing that she was still dressed.

It was on the tip of Damaris's tongue to refuse Sara, but if Robert were to find the girl, he might make her the victim of his temper. "Very well, but hurry, and we'll need to be very quiet. I am counting on the fact that this house is seamed with passageways."

"It is that, miss." Sara nodded solemnly. She slipped on her shoes hurriedly and took her cloak from its peg as Damaris opened the door quietly. The two young women emerged cautiously and started down the hall. They had gone several paces when Damaris came to a stop, a cry muffled in her throat as she saw a tall shape moving toward them. Behind her, she heard Sara moan. Then, from some distance away, she heard another sound.

Someone was shouting her name, and in that same moment, she found herself face-to-face with Rafe!

"Missus," he began,

"Shhhhh," she breathed. "Can you show us how we may leave without the...gentleman seeing us?"

Rafe, bless him, did not ask any unnecessary questions. He said merely, "The backstairs, missus. They be down this way."

"Can you take us to Mrs. Proctor's house?"

"Yes, missus. You'll have to watch yer step on them stairs, missus. They be very steep."

Over a heart which was in her throat, Damaris whispered, "We will."

They were not only steep, they also creaked. With each sound, Damaris feared Robert would find their location and come after them, but they reached the bottom without such untoward interference, and moments later they were in the passage leading to the yard.

As they emerged outside, Damaris was visited by another memory. "The stables aren't far from here," she said with certainty.

"No, missus." Rafe jerked a thumb toward the left.

"Are there any horses?"

"There be my old Betsy, 'n' there be the gentleman's horse wot I stabled."

Damaris clutched his arm. "'Tis best we take both. I'll see you have your Betsy back once we're at the inn."

Rafe nodded. "I'll saddle 'er up, missus." He added with a knowing grin, "Yon gentleman can't go far wi'out his horse."

Damaris could not conceal an answering grin. "'Tis very true, Rafe." She added, "But I'd not have him catch his death in the rain—so if he chooses, he may remain. I'll tell Mrs. Proctor but 'twill be better if you remain away and avoid his anger. I fear he'll be very upset when he finds his horse gone."

"I be too simple to be payin' heed to that, missus."
Another grin was written large upon Rafe's countenance.

Damaris was hard put not to throw her arms around
him and hug him. Rafe was a jewel. Still, she had best
remember that they were not safe yet. "Let us hurry,"
she urged.

Once in the stables, Damaris's admiration for Rafe
increased as the boy found an old sidesaddle for Robert's
horse and quickly made the change. Fortunately, Sara
was quite content to ride astride. She was clambering
onto Betsy's broad back when they heard footsteps
crunching on the gravel beyond the open door.

It was then that Rafe gave the real lie to Robert's
disparaging comments. Springing into the saddle behind
Sara, he put an arm around the girl and whispered to
Damaris, "Let's go." He urged his horse forward, and
the elderly animal took off with surprising speed.

Clattering after them, Damaris had a brief glimpse of
Robert's furious face. He made a dash for his appropri-
ated mount, only to fall back cursing as Damaris avoided
him easily and rode into the rain-swept twilight. Yet, as
she went, tears mingled with the drops spattering against
her cheeks. She had remembered a little lad who had
come to stare at her when she was first led into the great
hall at Harwine Keep.

"Who are you?" he had demanded.

"I'm D'maris Vardon," she had whispered, looking
with wide, frightened eyes at her vast and unfamiliar
surroundings.

"I'm Robert Harwine," he had said. "Are you going
to be my friend?"

"Oh, yes."

"Good, I'll be your friend, too. Forever and ever."

Damaris blinked and rode swiftly after Rafe and Sara
down the road to the caretaker's house.

CHAPTER
Ten

THE LUMBERING OLD stagecoach from York lurched into the courtyard of the Black Swan Tavern in London and came to a shuddering stop. Damaris, squeezed between a large lady who smelled strongly of brandy and peppermints and a thin solicitor's clerk, exchanged a speaking glance with Sara, who was pressed between an unpleasant old lady with a hacking cough and an enormously fat merchant whose boisterous laugh rang out far too often and whose small, mean eyes had wandered over the abigail's body far too often during the interminable journey.

Not even the fact that the rain, which had traveled with them for the two hundred odd miles that stretched between the Border and London, was still pelting down, dampened their pleasure at having finally arrived at their destination. It was only when they were settled in a hackney that Damaris, when asked her direction, experienced some panic. Her resources were much depleted and since the journey to Somerset still lay before her, she had not the funds for a good hostelry. She was loath to venture into such poor accommodations as her purse would allow. Of course, she could call upon Mary, but she doubted she could refrain from giving that silly creature the rough side of her tongue. Evidently some part of her quandary was visible in her expression for Sara said shyly, "Beggin' yer pardon, miss, but mightn't we go to the 'ouse?"

"The house, Sara?" Damaris questioned.

"Ought to be old Carlson at the 'ouse. 'Arewine 'ouse, miss."

"Carlson . . ." Damaris frowned. She was having difficulty gathering her thoughts. "Ah, the caretaker. Why yes, he should be . . . must be there. And 'twould only be for a night or two at the most." She bit down a feeling of panic. Until that moment she had been entertaining only one idea—she longed to seek out Giles and beg his pardon. Now other very troubling reflections were crowding into her head. She feared that he would be both angry and hurt at her hasty and ill-considered conclusions. It would be a painful interview, at best, and she could not even begin to envision its outcome. It might be well if she had an extra day or two to amass her arguments.

"Ah, miss," the driver said, "where be you a-goin'?" As if to emphasize an eagerness to be underway, he gave his reins a shake, causing his horses to respond with a forward movement.

With an apologetic smile, Damaris gave him the direction of Harwine House.

The mansion appeared singularly uninviting, Damaris thought dolefully as she and Sara came up to the tall iron gates. The windows were shuttered and, though the rain had momentarily ceased, water dripped from the roof, and deep puddles lay on either side of the flagstoned walk. It would probably be damp and cold inside. She doubted that Carlson would have built any fires in the drawing room or parlor.

"Miss Damaris!" Sara exclaimed in surprise. "One of these 'ere gates be open."

Damaris was dismayed as well as surprised. When the family was not in residence, the gates always remained locked and a bell was rung to summon the caretaker. He had served the family for many years, she recalled. Perhaps he was growing old and forgetful. Pushing the gate back, she started up the walk toward the door. An inadvertent glance at the windows above her reminded her of the pebbles Robert had been wont to fling, but she quickly banished what threatened to be a parade of unhappy memories. Arriving at the stoop, she raised and let fall the knocker, and in that same moment she was seized by panic. What if Carlson were not there?

Again her thoughts must have been mirrored in her face for Sara said, "Lord, I 'ope 'e be to home."

"I hope so, too." Damaris nodded. On an impulse she did not even understand, she turned the doorknob. To her surprise and alarm, the door swung back.

"Ooooh, Miss Damaris," Sara gasped. "It be open!"

Damaris found herself sharing Sara's obvious fears, but it would not do to add to them by letting the girl know of her trepidation. Lifting her chin, she stepped determinedly inside and glanced warily about her. She half-expected to find the table in the entrance hall denuded of its silver card tray and its heavy silver candlesticks, but all were there. Still, the footpads might be prowling about the house. She gazed apprehensively toward the stairs and stiffened, while behind her came Sara's terrified moan as she, too, must have caught sight of the tall, thin figure in white that had suddenly descended to the first landing. In the gray light issuing from the long window to its left, it looked almost spectral.

"Oh, my lord, ye must come back," old Carlson's quavering tones reached them. "Ye must come back to bed."

In a voice so cracked and hoarse it was painful to hear, the apparition rasped, "Mus' find her . . . mus' find her."

The caretaker came into view in the same moment that Damaris shrieked, "Giles!" and rushed up the stairs.

"Miss Damaris!" The caretaker came to a standstill and regarded her incredulously. "Oh, Miss Damaris, 'e's been lookin' for ye . . . come 'ere last night . . . wanted to go out straightaways . . . wouldn't listen to me . . . 'ad to knock 'im down an' put 'im to bed."

Damaris hardly heard him. Her horrified gaze remained on Giles—a Giles she barely recognized. In a little over two weeks, he had grown thin and gaunt. A rough stubble of beard coated his cheeks, and his eyes were red-rimmed and bloodshot.

Tears flooded her eyes. "Oh, Giles, my very dearest," she whispered.

"Mus' find her," Giles croaked, staring at her blankly. "Mus' find D'maris."

"Oh, miss," Sara shrilled, "wot be the matter wi' 'im?"

"'Tis a fever. 'E be burnin' up 'n I daren't leave 'im alone or 'e'll be gettin' out again." The caretaker panted, his old face creased with worry. "'E already done it once."

"Mus' find . . ." Giles started down the stairs.

Coming out of her half-daze, Damaris hastily stretched out restraining hands and pushed Giles back, while Carlson seized his arm. "We must get him to his chamber," she said crisply. "You keep tight hold of him, Carlson, and I'll take his other arm. You stand in back of him, Sara."

" 'E be powerful strong, Miss Damaris," the caretaker warned.

"Surely he's not so strong that he can contend against the three of us," she returned equably. "Now come. And hurry. He should not be here in this cold hall."

Five minutes later Damaris, standing at the foot of Giles's bed, clutched at a post. She had finally caught her breath. Returning the delirious man to his room had not been an easy chore. He had fought them furiously and now, at her direction, the caretaker and Sara had just finished tying him down with a rope the old man had found. That, too, had been difficult, for Giles had threshed about incessantly. He was still straining against his bonds as he continued to mutter, "Mus' find her."

Yet, even as she watched, that fever-augmented strength seemed to fail him for suddenly he sank back on his pillows and lay very still. Too still, Damaris thought fearfully. Hurrying to his side, she stared anxiously down at him. Much to her relief, he was still breathing. Bending over him, she started to brush his damp, tangled curls away from his forehead and exclaimed in horror. His skin was terribly hot to the touch. She turned urgently to the caretaker. "Bring cloths and fill the ewer with water," she ordered, pushing a chair close to the bed and sitting down.

Carlson looked at her with a ludicrous mixture of relief and apprehension. " 'E wouldn't be a-wantin' you in 'is room, miss."

" 'Tis no time to consider the proprieties, Carlson," she retorted. "Do as I say, please."

The old man's dubious expression was replaced by one of grudging respect. He picked up the ewer and left the room. Turning to Sara, Damaris said, "I think there's a bottle of cologne in my room. Will you fetch it for me, please?"

"Yes, miss." Sara hurried away.

Once Damaris was alone, the tears she had been blinking away poured down her cheeks. Giles's pallor frightened her, and surely he must have lost more than a stone since she had last seen him. "'Tis all my fault," she whispered, shaking her head.

Mindful of his duties as guardian, he had been searching for her—yet why had he not come to the Hall? Surely Mary would have told him where she had gone. She tensed. She had made Mary promise she would divulge nothing. Still, that had not kept her from confiding in Robert. She firmed her lips. Giles would have been a different matter. Mary was probably still seething over the night she had been locked in her chamber—and its aftermath. To Mary, Giles was "the enemy." Damaris suddenly knew that Mary would have exacted her revenge by telling him nothing—or, worse yet, sending him off in the wrong direction.

"Oh, my poor darling," she murmured and then tensed as his eyes suddenly opened wide.

"Damaris," he whispered.

"Giles, my dearest," she breathed. "I . . ." She paused as he moved restlessly on his pillow.

"Mus' find her, mus', mus'," he groaned and broke into a violent fit of coughing.

Damaris regarded him with horror. Each cough seemed wrenched from his chest, and in its wake his whole body shivered and shook. He was ill—even more ill than she had realized. He might even be sick unto death.

"No," she groaned. Leaning forward, she put her arms around him and held him protectively. "No, no, no," she said fiercely, "I shan't let you die, my own darling. I shan't let it happen."

Two hours later, Damaris had cause to remember that frantic vow. At her request, the caretaker had fetched Mr. Farnall, the physician who had attended both Lord and Lady Harwine during their final illnesses. Standing outside of the sickroom while he examined Giles, Damaris reluctantly remembered similar moments during Lord Harwine's times of crisis. She found herself repeating, "Not again...not again," while she wondered what was taking the doctor so very long to make his diagnosis. She wished that she had been allowed to remain with Giles, but Mr. Farnall's shocked look had made it quite impossible for her to explain that she had already performed services of a nature equal to the intimacies of a mere physical examination. Now, as she waited for the doctor, she was perilously close to telling him what she thought of his absurd scruples. The sentences were forming on her tongue as he emerged from Giles's room but one look at his grave face dissolved them into nothing.

"Well?" she whispered.

The doctor sighed and shook his head. "He's a very sick man. 'Tis obvious that there are a great many impurities in his blood, and the sooner 'tis drawn—"

"No!" Damaris cried. "I'll not have it."

The doctor regarded her with anger and amazement. "What do you say?"

"I will not allow him to be bled," she said firmly. "I yet remember how weak his father was after such treatments. In fact—" Meeting Farnall's choleric glance, she did not finish the rest of the sentence, implying that his treatment may have hastened Lord Harwine's end. She merely repeated, "I will not allow it."

"You have not the authority," the doctor began huffily.

"On the contrary," she returned calmly, "I do have the authority. I stand surrogate for Lord Harwine's other relations."

The doctor drew himself up. "You take a good deal upon yourself, Miss Vardon."

"I will bear the responsibility," she replied steadily.

"You may not bear it long."

She swallowed a lump in her throat. There was no mistaking his meaning, but she must stand firm. "I will take the chance."

He was silent a moment. Then, inclining his head, he said, "As you choose, Miss Vardon. But you must understand that in these circumstances I will not be able to attend the patient."

"I understand," she replied with a calmness she was far from feeling.

"We will . . . hope for his recovery," the doctor said dubiously. Wheeling, he made her a short bow and stalked from the room.

Damaris fled back into Giles's bedchamber. Mercifully, he had fallen asleep. Picking up the candle that stood on the table near his bed, she held it high over his face. He was yet so very pale. If he had lost blood . . .

"I know I am right, my very dearest," she whispered into his unheeding ears. "Please, God, I am right," she added fearfully and, resuming her seat by his bedside, she dipped a cloth into the basin that also stood on the table and pressed it against Giles's forehead.

Damaris sat at an embroidery frame in the second drawing room of Harwine House. She was working on a garland of roses—pink roses on a dark blue background. Thousands and thousands of stitches later, she would have a chair cover.

But her heart was not really in her work. It was only something to occupy her time since Cousin Phoebe had arrived and expelled her from Giles's chamber, saying in her scolding tones, "I cannot think what he would do were he ever to learn of your attendance upon him, my child."

That had been a fortnight earlier—the day after Giles had finally passed the crisis. A spent and weary Damaris had been able to assure her outraged chaperone that Giles would not remember the exigencies of the past ten days. Once his fever had broken, he had fallen into a deep and mercifully healing slumber. He had awakened to find Cousin Phoebe knitting at his bedside. That lady had subsequently assured Damaris that she had been right.

"And 'tis just as well he does not remember, my dear. Surely it would distress him greatly, given his strong sense of propriety," she had said sternly.

Damaris was in wry agreement with her. Had Giles known of her constant attendance upon him before he had taken a turn for the better, he might well have suffered a relapse. Still, considering the reasons for that same illness, it was very odd that he had not asked to see her. Of course, he had been very weak, and had, in fact, remained in his bed for another five days. However, in the last three days, he had been up for the greater part of the morning and some of the afternoon, dividing his time between library and back parlor. Yet, she could comfort herself that, aside from Peake, Travers, and Carlson, he had seen no one, not even his concerned and repentant sister Mary, who, as Damaris had feared, had sent him off to Cornwall in search of her.

However, he had forgiven Mary. She had had the story from that lady, herself. At Mary's urging, she had also promised not to tell Giles what had taken place at the castle. She was glad of that—if only for the sake of Robert's bride, whom he had now joined. They were on their way back to Canada. Cousin Phoebe had told Damaris in deeply disapproving tones that Giles had sent word to his man of business to provide a large quarterly allowance for Robert on the condition that he remain in the New World.

"Let him set foot on this shore and 'twill cease," Cousin Phoebe had said with some scant satisfaction. "Considering all the trouble that young scapegrace has created, 'twould be better to have let him remain in the Fleet. Indeed, I am certain that, if there's a similar facility in America, 'twill not be long before he's in it."

Cousin Phoebe had been almost as critical of Damaris. "'Twas all your fault," she had said coldly, "leading poor Giles such a dance from one end of the country to the other in all weather. 'Tis no wonder he nearly died."

Damaris blinked away a tear. Once more she pictured him tossing and turning in his bed, pulling away from her when she had sought to soothe him. She winced. There had been one terrible night when she had truly believed he must die. Climbing onto his bed, she had lain close beside him, clutching his quivering body. "Come back, my dearest darling. You cannot leave me, not when I love you with all my heart," she had moaned. Oddly enough, there had been a moment when it had seemed as if he were actually listening to her, listening and understanding, but then he had lapsed into wild and incomprehensible speech. Later that night there had been the crisis and afterward that blessed healing slumber.

Damaris smiled, glad that dreadful period was ended— glad, too, that she had been proved right about Giles's treatment. Another younger doctor, who had come to tend him, had told her that, in his opinion, bloodletting might have caused his death. "His strength would have gone with it, ma'am."

Damaris started and pricked her finger with the needle as the candle by her side flared at a draft from an open door. She did not look up. She had begged Cousin Phoebe to ask Giles a question. She must have returned with the answer. "Will he see me, yet?" she demanded in a low voice.

"Yes, he will see you, Damaris."

The needle dropped from her fingers. Damaris raised amazed eyes to the tall, pale man who stood in the doorway. "Giles!" She rushed to his side. "Oh, you are out of your room and 'tis snowing." She pointed to the flake-covered windows.

"'Tis not snowing in here," he said.

"Still, it is drafty. At least sit near the fire. I shall put more wood upon it, for 'tis burning low."

He gave her one of his old, grave smiles. "My dear Damaris, I am quite myself again. How could I not be when I have had such excellent nursing?"

Much to her confusion, Damaris felt her cheeks grow warm. She looked down quickly. "Cousin Phoebe is a fine nurse," she murmured.

"She is," he agreed. "I owe her a great deal."

"Yes, you do. But I beg you'll sit down," she insisted.

"Very well." He moved to the sofa.

Damaris eyed him anxiously. He was breathing hard. "I cannot think you should have left the library, where 'tis much warmer than here," she said worriedly.

"I would rather be here," he returned, adding, "Will you sit near me? I wish to talk to you, and 'tis yet difficult for me to shout."

"Of course," Damaris agreed with a touch of disappointment. She had hoped against hope that he wanted her to be near him for a different reason. But how could that be when all he remembered was the day she had fled his house without giving him a chance to explain anything. If only she had waited!

"Damaris." Giles bent a serious look upon her, as she took her seat on the couch. "I am most concerned about—"

"About my running away?" she interrupted. Earnestly and, at the same time apologetically, she continued, "I wish you to know that it was not long before I realized I was wrong to believe that you had...had any connection with that girl. But at the time she made herself so very much at home and spoke so knowingly about so many things connected with the family and the estate—"

"That was Robert's doing," Giles interrupted grimly.

"But Cousin Phoebe has told me that you know all about his duplicity."

"I do," Damaris said. "And so must his . . . wife, though Mary says she has been spared the tale of our near-elopement. I am glad of that. She must be unhappy enough already at the way she was deceived."

"She was confused," Giles emphasized. He sighed. "'Twas poor payment for the way she and her family nursed him back to health once he'd escaped from prison."

"He spoke of a farm family," Damaris said in some surprise. "She did not seem like a farm girl."

"Nor is she. His tale was a great tissue of lies and half-truths. He was sheltered by farm folk who worked on her father's estate. When Robert came to them, they told their master. He and his daughter went to see him and were much impressed by his elegance of manner. They brought him to their house—where, upon his revealing that he was Lord Harwine . . ."

"A memory lapse, no doubt?" Damaris interrupted with a lift of her eyebrow.

A spark of humor flickered in Giles's eyes. "One of his few, I fear." The spark turned into a gleam. "Otherwise he told her things about our family that even I'd forgotten. No doubt it would surprise you to know, Damaris, that 'twas a Harwine—not King Henry V—who trounced the French at Agincourt!"

"He did not say such a thing!" Damaris cried.

"He did . . . and then there was the Robert Harwine who sailed with Drake, and the Harwine who aided Charles II in escaping from our shores. He told her so many tales about our illustrious kindred that she could not wait to see our ancestral acres. She determined to take ship and surprise him, which she did soon after receiving his first letter."

"Poor thing. Was she much cast down when she heard the truth?"

Giles shook his head and sighed. "I was hard put to

make her believe me and when she did at length realize
that I was Lord Harwine, she promptly forgave Robert."

"So quickly?" Damaris stared at him incredulously.

An ironical smile twisted Giles's lips. "She believed
'twas done because, being so heart-smitten—her words,
not mine—he was determined to impress her. She was
sorry for him and even more fond, I think, than before.
My brother has a way with women."

"Until they know him for what he is," Damaris said
tartly. "For her sake, I pray she remains in ignorance."
A memory of what she had almost endured at Robert's
hands arose to confront her and vanished immediately as
she looked at Giles. It seemed to her that he was breathing
far too rapidly, and there were spots of color in his pale
cheeks which, to her worried eye, suggested a return of
his fever. She was about to beg that he return to his
bedchamber when he bent a frowning gaze upon her.

"My dear," he said, "there's something that yet troubles me. I have a distinct memory of you sitting at my
bedside during my illness, but Cousin Phoebe assures
me 'twas delirium."

Damaris feared she was blushing. "Oh, it was," she
assured him hastily.

"Ah, that is good. Else I should be much concerned
by attentions that were hardly those a young woman
ought to provide for one who was neither relation nor
husband."

Damaris looked down at the carpet. "I expect you are
right."

"About what?"

She found that question confusing. "Those attentions," she murmured, still not looking at him.

"Which were not of your providing. And 'twas not
your voice that called me back to life when I would have
given up out of despair for having lost you when I love
you with all my heart?"

"Giles!" Damaris raised astonished eyes to his face.

He seized her hand. "Dare you tell me that it was Cousin Phoebe's voice I heard? And was it Cousin Phoebe's arms that held me?"

Despite his illness, his grip was strong and warm on her hand. Her heart was beating very fast. She shook her head. "No," she said very softly. "I dare not tell you such a . . . a falsehood."

"Ah," he breathed. "Why did you lie to me, then?"

"Because . . . because of the proprieties." She faltered. "You have always set such . . . such store by them, and Cousin Phoebe s-said and I agreed that you'd be most upset and . . . and angry if you were to learn that . . ."

"That you had saved my life?" he said softly, tenderly. "Damaris." He caught her other hand. His green eyes glowed as he gazed at her. "Can you not guess why I was always so adamant in that regard? Do you not know that the proprieties were my only protection?"

"P-Protection?" she questioned in amazement.

"Protection," he repeated. "For you and for myself. Without that barrier, I did not trust myself, and I wanted to be fair, even though I had loved you such a long time."

"You had?" she whispered incredulously.

"For years." He sighed.

"But Lady Laura—"

"Was foolish, reckless and, alas, all-too-easily forgotten, my own."

"And was I not foolish?" Damaris murmured, "going about in black mainly to . . . to spite you." She hung her head. "I think I loved you even then. I began to realize how much I cared about you on the day of the naumachia, and before Robert came back I was sure of it. But you were so distant . . . and you'd told me to make a good marriage to . . . someone else and . . . I felt sorry for R-Robert and . . . you had hurt me so dreadfully."

"Oh, God," he groaned, "what else could I do? I was your guardian. I hated that position—but there was nothing I could do about it. I thought it was not fair to take advantage of you. You'd locked yourself away for so long that you'd known only Robert and myself."

"Oh, Giles." She unleashed a long, quavering sigh. "If you only knew how very long I have wanted you to—to take advantage of me. I do love you so very much. In fact, I wish now that—" She broke off, flushing.

"What do you wish, my angel?" His green eyes were shining, and he was very close to her.

"I wish something that is not in the least angelic." She smiled mistily. "I want you to—to take advantage of me, now . . . this very second."

His gentle, happy laughter filled her ears. "I will, my love. Directly."

"Directly?" she questioned with a tiny frown.

"Directly we are wed, my own."

"Oh." She wound her arms around his neck. "But that is such a long time to wait."

He shook his head. "Not so long. I can procure a special license, and, if you have no objections to a very quiet wedding, it could take place as early as this evening. He put his arms around her. "What do you say to that?"

Damaris pressed close against him and put her lips to his ear. "I say only one thing." She paused.

"And what is that, my darling?"

"I have no objections whatsoever."

All of the above titles are $1.75 per copy

_____ 06851-9 A MAN'S PERSUASION #89 Katherine Granger

_____ 06852-7 FORBIDDEN RAPTURE #90 Kate Nevins

_____ 06853-5 THIS WILD HEART #91 Margarett McKean

_____ 06854-3 SPLENDID SAVAGE #92 Zandra Colt

_____ 06855-1 THE EARL'S FANCY #93 Charlotte Hines

_____ 06858-6 BREATHLESS DAWN #94 Susanna Collins

_____ 06859-4 SWEET SURRENDER #95 Diana Mars

_____ 06860-8 GUARDED MOMENTS #96 Lynn Fairfax

_____ 06861-6 ECSTASY RECLAIMED #97 Brandy LaRue

_____ 06862-4 THE WIND'S EMBRACE #98 Melinda Harris

_____ 06863-2 THE FORGOTTEN BRIDE #99 Lillian Marsh

_____ 06864-0 A PROMISE TO CHERISH #100 LaVyrle Spencer

_____ 06865-9 GENTLE AWAKENING #101 Marianne Cole

_____ 06866-7 BELOVED STRANGER #102 Michelle Roland

_____ 06867-5 ENTHRALLED #103 Ann Cristy

_____ 06868-3 TRIAL BY FIRE #104 Faye Morgan

_____ 06869-1 DEFIANT MISTRESS #105 Anne Devon

_____ 06870-5 RELENTLESS DESIRE #106 Sandra Brown

_____ 06871-3 SCENES FROM THE HEART #107 Marie Charles

_____ 06872-1 SPRING FEVER #108 Simone Hadary

_____ 06873-X IN THE ARMS OF A STRANGER #109 Deborah Joyce

_____ 06874-8 TAKEN BY STORM #110 Kay Robbins

_____ 06899-3 THE ARDENT PROTECTOR #111 Amanda Kent

_____ 07200-1 A LASTING TREASURE #112 Cally Hughes $1.95

_____ 07201-X RESTLESS TIDES #113 Kelly Adams $1.95

_____ 07202-8 MOONLIGHT PERSUASION #114 Sharon Stone $1.95

_____ 07203-6 COME WINTER'S END #115 Claire Evans $1.95

_____ 07204-4 LET PASSION SOAR #116 Sherry Carr $1.95

_____ 07205-2 LONDON FROLIC #117 Josephine Janes $1.95

_____ 07206-0 IMPRISONED HEART #118 Jasmine Craig $1.95

_____ 07207-9 THE MAN FROM TENNESSEE #119 Jeanne Grant $1.95

_____ 07208-7 LAUGH WITH ME, LOVE WITH ME #120 Lee Damon $1.95

_____ 07209-5 PLAY IT BY HEART #121 Vanessa Valcour $1.95

_____ 07210-9 SWEET ABANDON #122 Diana Mars $1.95

_____ 07211-7 THE DASHING GUARDIAN #123 Lucia Curzon $1.95

All of the above titles are $1.75 per copy except where noted

WHAT READERS SAY ABOUT
SECOND CHANCE AT LOVE BOOKS

"Your books are the greatest!"
—*M. N., Carteret, New Jersey**

"I have been reading romance novels for quite some time, but the SECOND CHANCE AT LOVE books are the most enjoyable."
—*P. R., Vicksburg, Mississippi**

"I enjoy SECOND CHANCE [AT LOVE] more than any books that I have read and I do read a lot."
—*J. R., Gretna, Louisiana**

"I really think your books are exceptional... I read Harlequin and Silhouette and although I still like them, I'll buy your books over theirs. SECOND CHANCE [AT LOVE] is more interesting and holds your attention and imagination with a better story line..."
—*J. W., Flagstaff, Arizona**

"I've read many romances, but yours take the 'cake'!"
—*D. H., Bloomsburg, Pennsylvania**

"Have waited ten years for *good* romance books. Now I have them."
—*M. P., Jacksonville, Florida**

*Names and addresses available upon request